PRAISE FOR WE

- Finalist, the Eric Hoffer Award for Short Prose and Independent Books
- Bronze Medal, ForeWord Magazine Book of the Year Award, General Fiction category
- Winner, ForeWord Magazine's quarterly Debut Novelist Award

★ ★ ★ ★ ★ "Reflective and introspective, yet highly charged with dramatic scenes in a race against time, this mesmerizing novel is a page-turner that will captivate even a jaded critic…. As Ben interacts with Binky in this touching and often humorous tale, the far-fetched aspect of this unusual occurrence is accepted. Drawn into the warring conversation between adult and child—parts of the same personality— one will learn what constitutes real maturity opposed to merely grown-up behavior when a sibling's life is threatened. Striking is the dual perspective within the same protagonist, an unusual angle that can be difficult to implement…. [In *We*, Landweber] makes not only an impressive debut, but has already succeeded at an experimental undertaking few could achieve."
—Julia Ann Charpentier, ForeWord Clarion Reviews

"Landweber apparently approached this project with a go-big-or-go-home attitude. He aimed high and hit the mark, pulling off a fusion of literary novel and psychological drama."
—Tom Young, *The Washington Independent Review of Books*

"*We* is a family story at its heart, wrapped in a suspenseful, gripping, and totally original sci fi narrative. The unforgettable double consciousness will keep you up reading until the emotionally gratifying end."
—Jessica Anya Blau, author of *The Wonder Bread Summer*

"What if we could change the past? What if the past didn't necessarily want to change? Michael Landweber's *We* is part sci-fi concept novel, part psychological thriller with literary edges: Landweber deftly weaves time travel, Jungian psychology, and the butterfly effect into a suspenseful but also emotionally engaging novel."
—Jen Michalski, author of *The Tide King*

"*We* is a captivating, genre-bending psychological mystery that's equal parts *It's a Wonderful Life* and *The Twilight Zone*."
—Dave Housley, author of *Ryan Seacrest is Famous*

"Landweber writes beautifully, with soaring imagination, heart and soul …. *We* is a wonderful mix of psychological thriller, science fiction, and love story—love of self, love of family, love of life. I find myself at a loss for words (a rare thing) when describing the beauty and profound meaning of this novel. It has touched me deeply. It should be on every bestseller list."
—Claudia Sparks, Mockingbird Hill Cottage Blog

"Ultimately, We is about a man struggling with his own inner demons and failures while occupying the mind of his younger self, hoping to reverse time and alter a devastating outcome. Will he succeed? If he does, what will the implications be? These questions will be answered by the end of the book, as Landweber leaves the reader with the satisfied sense that no stone was left unturned. If you ask me, there is truly nothing better in life than getting lost in a good book

as time stands still, and that's exactly what happened when I read We by Michael Landweber from cover to cover in a day. If you read one book this Spring, make it We. You won't regret it."
—Allison Hiltz, The Book Wheel

"[*We*] is totally unlike anything I have read…. The writing is tight and vibrant. The ambiance of confusion is very well recreated …. So if you want to read something different and unusual, and are ready for a confusing adventure outside your comfort zone, you will enjoy *We*."
—Emma, Words and Peace Blog

"An intriguing story as well as one that showcases Landweber's obvious talents as a writer."
—No More Grumpy Bookseller Blog

"Thought-provoking, touching, imaginative …. a promising debut."
—Gayle Weisswasser, Everyday I Write the Book Blog

THURSDAY 1:17 PM

THURSDAY 1:17 PM

A Novel

Michael Landweber

coffeetownpress

Seattle, WA

coffeetownpress

Coffeetown Press
PO Box 70515
Seattle, WA 98127

For more information go to: www.coffeetownpress.com
www.mikelandweber.com

This is a work of fiction. Names, characters, places, brands, media, and incidents are either the product of the author's imagination or are used fictitiously.

Cover design by Sabrina Sun

ISBN: 978-1-60381-357-0 (Trade Paper)
ISBN: 978-1-60381-358-7 (eBook)

Library of Congress Control Number: 2015957527

Printed in the United States of America

In memory of Lenore Flory

Acknowledgments

THANKS TO CATHERINE, JENNIFER, and everyone else at Coffeetown for helping to bring my second novel to life and making it such an enjoyable experience.

As always, I greatly appreciate the many writers and editors who have taken time to encourage and help me improve my work over the years—Jen Michalski, Susi Wyss, Julie Wakeman-Linn, Dave Housley, Amber Sparks, Richard Peabody, Jessica Anya Blau, Mark Cugini, Bryn Greenwood, and Michelle Brafman, just to name a few.

Thanks to Mrs. Travis, for not only helping me learn how to write, but more importantly teaching me how to edit.

A particular thanks to the book group—Bonnie Lo, Elana Tyrangiel, Leigh Lipson, Flo Kao, Kate Haley Goldman—for reading an early draft of the book and giving me their thoughts.

Also, I have been lucky enough to have a strong and supportive (and extensive) family cheering me on with every new book. Thanks to all the Landwebers, Florys, Capras, Hofmanns, Senreiches, Phillipses, Benders, Greenhouses, Siffs, Fosters and others for getting behind whatever craziness comes out of my head and ends up on the page. And that goes double for Gillian, Josh, and Maya.

Also by the author

We

Contents

Thursday, 1:17 p.m.

TIME STOPPED WHILE I was crossing the street at the intersection of Jenifer and Wisconsin Avenue. It was 1:17 p.m. on a Thursday. End of May. The D.C. summer heat hadn't kicked in yet. Sunny and 71 degrees. My frozen world was downright balmy.

I was going somewhere. I had no idea where. But I needed to get out of the house because that's where my dead mother was. And I didn't know where to go. I had my music on. Loud. I was crying.

So I had put on the mix I made for my mom. All '80s, all the time. Not the crappy '80s, but the '80s that she loved. She was one of the few people who would argue that the '80s was the pinnacle of music. Screw the Beatles and Stones. Forget Zep and Pink Floyd. Don't even bring up hip-hop or country or classical or whatever. My mother loved The Clash and Talking Heads and the English Beat and Elvis Costello and The Specials and those first few U2 albums and all those bands that now get lumped together under the bizarre grouping of Classic Adult Alternative. When she was only a little bit sick, I created Mom's Sick Mix. Here's the thing: I told her I was using "sick" like awesome, not "sick" like diseased, but after a while I started to feel like it was just "sick" in the head, but that was even worse because she had a brain tumor, which really was sick in the head.

All of this was going through my mind as I stormed down the street, angry at everything, not paying attention because nothing really mattered anyway.

The next part I'm kind of making up because I might have mentioned that I wasn't paying attention. But here goes. I stepped off the curb into the street. I didn't realize the light hadn't changed. I didn't hear the car barreling toward me, trying to make it through the intersection on the yellow. I didn't hear the people shouting for me to get out of the way. I didn't realize that I was about to die.

Then, the music stopped.

I was listening to "Begin the Begin." R.E.M. Not a bad last song. If you've got to have something stuck in your head forever with no real possibility of another song coming along randomly to shove it aside, well then, it might as well be some R.E.M. from an early album.

I fingered my phone, trying different combinations of swiping and poking to get it working again. Nothing. It pissed me off that I'd probably have to go to the Apple Store in Bethesda to get it fixed. But it also distracted me for a moment, from where I was going and what I was trying to leave behind. Standing in the middle of the street, all I could hear was the last bars echoing in my head.

Another song that might have been better: "Stuck In A Moment You Can't Get Out Of." U2. Yeah, that would have been funny.

The Mercedes had stopped inches from me. Dead frozen forever stopped. Still distracted by the malfunctioning phone, my brain was slow to process the car. It was way too close. If it had come to a stop that abruptly, I would have heard the screeching of the brakes. I should have flinched. Or maybe

I was so out of it that I nearly walked into the stopped car. And then there was the problem of the engine. No sound. I wondered if it was a hybrid.

I looked at the driver. His face would make it clear if this was his fault or mine. I was ready to pound on his hood or at least give him a dirty look if he seemed guilty. If he was angry, I'd lower my head and cross the street quickly, hoping he wouldn't get out of his car.

His face looked weird. I didn't know what to make of it.

The man's lower jaw jutted out and his lips curled back, exposing his teeth. His eyes were perfect circles, open as wide as possible. The muscles in his cheeks were tensed, pushing into his nose, which bent slightly to the left. His expression would have made a pretty scary Halloween mask. Terrified man frozen in time.

That's how I interpreted it. Fear, paramount. *I blew it. I'm going to hit this guy.* His body, reflexively, was trying to save him. I could see the steering wheel turned in his clutched white hands. The front wheels of the car followed, obliquely angled, ready to take it on a different path. Despite his best efforts, he would have hit me with the right side of his bumper. Anger mixed with the fear. His eyes bore down on me fiercely. How dare I step off the curb? A layer of regret, possibly—but that could be something I was seeing because I wanted to see it. I wanted him to be sorry for what he was about to do. I wanted him to feel the pain I was about to receive. And digging deeper—surprise, confusion, sadness.

The driver was clearly late. Why else would he be running the red? Maybe arrogance. Driving that expensive car, wearing that perfectly tailored suit—*I can make it,* he thought. Maybe he lost focus. Thinking about an important meeting. Or a fight with his wife. Maybe he had just gotten off his cellphone, looked up, and realized he was going too fast to stop. So he sped up. Or maybe not.

Meanwhile, I was background processing a far more

important observation. Nothing at that intersection was moving. Nothing except for me.

At first, I tried to be still too, wondering if I was about to be captured, fearing the very phenomenon that had just saved my life.

The man stared at me through the windshield, his bared teeth becoming more threatening by the moment. He looked like he wanted to eat me, like his face must hurt.

There was nothing for me to do but move.

Sometimes it is difficult to read expressions in a static world. The movement of muscles, the interplay of facial components, the momentum of emotion—all these things are absent. Everything is a still photograph, and those can be cryptic.

From the corner, three people watched. A bike messenger with dreadlocks and an oversized tote, his expression hidden behind wraparound sunglasses and hip facial hair. The car must have been coming pretty fast for a bike messenger with no respect for the laws of traffic or physics to wait patiently on the curb. Maybe he was looking forward to watching me die. *Better than YouTube, dude.* I knew I was not being fair to him, but compared to the two people standing next to him, he was complicit with the driver in my mind.

The second person—a young man in a button-down shirt and khakis, possibly on his way to a job interview, maybe going to grab a late lunch from his low-paying job at a non-profit—wanted to rescue me. He was in the process of raising his arm to point in my direction. His brow was furrowed and his mouth was partially open, ready to shout. This man quite possibly was about to dart out into the street to save my life.

But it was the woman next to him—early forties, light brown skin, wearing a business suit—who was the easiest to read. Her face a mask of shock and despair. Tears already formed in her eyes. She did not want to see what she knew was coming. It will devastate her, haunt her dreams and torture her days— watching a man die. Her faith would be tested and she would find no reason for my death except pure awful dumb luck.

Around that one intersection, there were dozens of other people—some in cars, some walking, the food truck guy leaning out the window and handing a taco to a teenager, a homeless guy sleeping on a bench, folks waiting for a bus. To varying degrees, they were all aware of what was about to happen, most of them more so than I was. Some had turned to look at me over their shoulders and would catch a glimpse of the accident but doubt their own recollection of it. Some would notice after the event, when I lay dying, a bloody carcass interrupting the normal course of their lives. Others would see it all, beginning to end, and feel powerless to prevent it, thankful it was not their day to take the blow.

I stumbled away from the Mercedes. There were no cars in the intersection itself. On Jenifer, the drivers had paused at the green, anticipating the Mercedes. And on Wisconsin, all the other vehicles had stopped on the red.

All the people continued to stare at the space I had occupied, the one I'd just vacated. Their expressions did not change. But I was gone. I had disappeared. Yet, they all still saw me there, about to get run over.

It felt safest to stand in the dead center of the intersection, away from all those living statues. I drifted there and waited for something to move. Anything. I turned myself into a statue too. Perfectly still. I didn't want to stand out. I didn't want to move.

I didn't want to be alone.

My cheeks still wet with tears, I fell to my knees and threw up. My body continued to be racked by dry heaves after the contents of my stomach had emptied onto the asphalt. No one came to comfort me. No one asked if I was okay. No one moved.

The smell of my vomit filled my nostrils, pummeling me with another wave of nausea. I couldn't stay there. So I ran. I didn't look at anyone or anything. I pretended that nothing had changed. I closed my eyes, and I ran.

And as I ran, snippets of "Begin the Begin" flickered in my mind, taunting me.

Miles Standish. Martin Luther. Something about grabbing a bird.

None of it made any sense.

Somewhere, Michael Stipe was frozen solid like everyone else. I wanted to find him and kick his ass for writing such cryptic lyrics.

None of this made any sense.

Note About This Guide to Your Frozen World

THIS GUIDE IS INTENDED to help those who find themselves in the unique situation in which the author currently finds himself. It is unlikely to discover much of an audience because the situation is, as stated in the first sentence, unique. If, in fact, this guide is ever read by anyone other than the author, and it actually is useful because the reader is in a similar (or even identical) situation, well, that would be surprising.

The method employed in this guide is first person narrative journalism, sort of like the author was exposed to during Mr. Halliwell's non-fiction writing seminar last year. Some might even call it confessional. Mr. Halliwell started off the first day by informing us that even though we were only sixteen we had a story to tell. He proceeded to have us analyze *The Electric Kool-Aid Acid Test* and *Fear and Loathing in Las Vegas* and *Zen and the Art of Motorcycle Maintenance*. "Now, what is your story?" he said.

The non-fiction writing seminar was one of the few classes where I was with Carlos and Grace—Carlos was pretty sure that Mr. Halliwell was trying to get us to smoke pot with him, which was probably true. Mr. Halliwell hasn't cut his hair or changed his wardrobe since 1975 and apparently that is also when he stopped buying new books. He is the kind of teacher who can only be found at certain types of private high schools that focus on instilling a vaguely liberal ethos of character and individuality. No nuns allowed. But it was one of the author's more interesting classes, and the lesson that non-fiction can also be quite surreal has informed the writing of this guide.

The author assures anyone who is reading this that the situations and circumstances described in this guide are real, not drug-induced hallucinations. Sorry, Mr. Halliwell.

This guide will on occasion be written in third person (as is almost consistently the case with this note). However, most of it will be in first person to fully capture the mise-en-scène. (Credit for that phrase goes to Ms. Yeardley, who is only a few years older than me, teaches European Cinema to seniors, thinks that Fellini was a hack compared to Bergman and may have been sleeping with one or more students—though surprisingly not Carlos. I'm pretty sure that both she and I have no idea what mise-en-scène really means.)

Throughout this guide, the reader (if there ever is one) will find that the usage of tenses is inconsistent. Past and present (though never, or rarely, future) tense will seem interchangeable. This is to be expected. Because, quite frankly, it is damn hard to tell the difference in the present situation.

Discussion: Sound

THE FIRST THING YOU will notice upon arriving in your frozen world is that there is no sound. Well, actually, the first thing you'll notice is that nothing moves at all, except you. You'll probably start screaming, which will delay your understanding that there is no sound. When you stop screaming, you will understand. And it will freak you out. Which is not surprising, because to be honest, everything about your frozen world should freak you out. If it doesn't, congratulations, you are a psychopath.

From this point forward, the only sounds you hear will be those that you yourself make. You can talk and shout and sing and wail. In the beginning, you will make noise just to remind yourself that you are still there. Other objects can make noise. But only if you intervene. You can bang on a drum and the thump is loud and clear. You can break a window and the initial crash is followed by the tinkling of shattered glass on the ground. If you throw a stone into a river, there will be a splash. The author has done all these things and more, because often it is really boring in the frozen world.

Let me tell you a story about sound.

Soon after the world stopped, I was convinced that I heard a plane. The loud roar of aircraft engines seemed to fill the world around me, mocking me as I ran madly through the streets scanning the sky for anything moving. An F-16. A helicopter. A prop plane. A 747. Anything to swoop down and save me from this fate.

I ended up on the shores of the Potomac, near the Kennedy Center. I could see across the river into Virginia along the approach route for planes flying into National Airport. A broad flight of stairs appears to dead end into the sky there, and joggers run up and down them all day, going nowhere. (I never understood why people want to run stairs, but they call it exercise and I guess I just have to accept that explanation.) A jogger ascended next to me, his foot in mid-air never to hit the next riser, beads of sweat like icy pearls on his forehead. I stared at a DC-9 dangling precariously on its approach, wondering how many people were in that plane and so many others frozen at thirty thousand feet, making no progress toward their destinations.

National has one of the scariest runways in the world. You come in right over the water. This plane appeared to be initiating a turn at the worst possible moment. It looked like it was about to bank into a fatal barrel roll. Of course, it was probably just a momentary buffeting of the wind, a microburst of air that led to this brief, and completely correctable, detour from its target. The pilot, if he ever has the chance, will gently tweak the stick and return the plane to a level heading and a perfect landing. The passengers feeling the slight bump will probably applaud, relieved. Of course, it could also be that a tragic error has been made. That plane could be going down. Maybe time stopped to prevent that crash.

I was still trying to determine where the roaring was coming from. "The ringing in my ears," I said out loud, my voice drowning it out long enough for me to realize that yes, that roaring was all in my head.

My ears had become self-referential. I was hearing the crash of the surf in a conch shell. Yours will too. With no outside stimuli, the eardrum, the cochlea, those three little bones, the nerves, with a generous assist from your reeling brain, will all turn their attention inward. Seeking out sounds, finding them in the workings of your body, which unlike the world around it is still a chaotic amalgam of movement and frantic activity. Blood courses through your veins, creating that dull roar in your head. Your heart still beats like a pile driver, especially when you panic, which will happen often. Air rushes in and out of lungs like a hurricane. Knuckles crack, intestines gurgle. Even the flutter of eyelashes whispers like a breeze through a weeping willow.

Notes About the Author and the Author's Friends

THE AUTHOR IS SEVENTEEN. Tomorrow is his eighteenth birthday. He will never be eighteen, given the circumstances.

He is the son of a philosopher and an archivist who referred to herself as a librarian. This genetic combination has adequately prepared the author to survive in the frozen world. He has also inherited traits from his parents that in normal society do not seem ideal, but are useful when you are stranded and alone. These include delusions of grandeur (Dad), borderline problematic organizational tendencies (Mom), and a functional ability to be happily alone (both).

According to the District of Columbia, the author is an orphan. As of today. Which is the only day. This would be a problem, bureaucratically, until tomorrow. Except that all the bureaucrats are frozen. And tomorrow is never coming. So I guess for the purposes of this guide, the author should be considered an emancipated minor. If tomorrow ever does arrive, there will be a whole different set of problems, because the author has no idea to handle those circumstances any better than the present ones.

It might be better to be alone than to figure out how to live alone.

The author's mother and father were both only children. So is the author. Before her condition deteriorated, the author's mother was trying to figure out who might take care of the author in the future. She hadn't come up with a good solution.

Luckily, that's not an issue in the frozen world. The author has no choice but to take care of himself. It's not like he isn't used to being abandoned by the adults who are supposed to be taking care of him, even when he knows that it isn't really their fault. He blames them anyway.

The author's mother died this morning. That's why the author was crossing the street at the corner of Wisconsin and Jenifer, bawling like a baby, listening to R.E.M. on his phone but really hoping someone would call him even though he was pretty sure no one would, when the world froze.

It's pretty pretentious to refer to yourself in the third person, but be warned I'll probably continue to do it. The author will too.

The author has friends. Not many, but enough. They call him Duck. Actually, everyone calls him Duck, which was originally meant as a provocation, but became a nickname thanks to Carlos, who pushed through a crowd of taunting kids on day one of the author's arrival at The Lab School for Gifted Children (Affiliated With George Washington University)— which will be known in this guide as LSGC(AWGWU)—and shut down the mob. He shook my hand and said he thought Duck was a pretty cool name.

Carlos Delgado is one of those people who has charisma up the yin-yang. Not many of them exist, even in this town full of the spawn of elected officials who owe all their success to charisma. To be fair, his parents *are* those people. His mom was a four-time congresswoman from Texas before she took her current position as the head of a center-left think tank.

Carlos' dad is a consultant who gets paid enormous amounts of money to tell politicians how Hispanics vote. As if the Delgado family was not rich and beautiful enough, you should see his three older sisters. Some of the author's happiest moments have been saying things like *hola chica* and *muy guapo* to one of the Delgado girls and having them laugh at his ridiculous accent.

As an aside, Carlos is aware that he shares a name with a famous baseball player. The author was not aware of this until middle school when it was pointed out to him; let's just say the author is not a sports fan. Carlos is named after his great grandfather, and as he will tell you is lucky that his last name is not Santana or The Jackal.

Why Carlos chose to save me that first day, I'll never know. When asked, he just says, you were cooler than them and they needed to know it. Why he is still friends with me, I also don't know, but I'm too afraid to ask that question. LSGC(AWGWU) is really small—only about fifty kids a grade in the high school—so we're all kind of friends. But Carlos is actually my real friend and it just doesn't make much sense. Sometimes these things don't. Maybe it did in elementary school, when none of us really knew our potential. But by middle school, he should have realized that he was a stud and I was a geek. Actually, what's great about Carlos is that he did realize it and it didn't matter to him.

But let's move on before this becomes too much of a Carlos Admiration Society. For the record, membership in the CAS is large and mostly female.

Grace Chang met the author in ninth grade, her first year at LSGC(AWGWU), when they became lab partners in biology. The author had difficulty with dissection, particularly one fetal pig that had inadvisably been dubbed Porky. Grace sliced it open, pulled the guts out and completed the assignment while the author tried not to gag. She is the daughter of two surgeons, so this should not have been surprising behavior.

Grace didn't have a Tiger Mom or Dad; they were too busy, so they outsourced her upbringing to a Tiger Nanny, a really scary German woman. It seems to have worked. Grace is going to Yale. She's spending her summer interning at the Natural History Museum, cataloguing mollusks and cephalopods. Except there won't be a summer, because the world is frozen, but Grace doesn't know that.

The author is a virgin. So is Grace. They have a pact that if they can't get laid in college, they'll sleep with each other. That's one of those things they don't share with Carlos, who is not a virgin and has slept with pretty much every girl at LSGC(AWGWU), though not Grace or Mackenzie.

There was a night in tenth grade when the author almost slept with Grace. They were alone in her house. They were bored. They started kissing and then things started moving fast and before they knew it, their shirts were off.

Maybe they didn't almost sleep together. They didn't know each other that well. The author was very scared. And Grace later told him that she was too. It is funny how sometimes things can just start happening and you just don't know where the brakes are. But in this case, the brakes were applied by the author's penis, which wilted when Grace touched it. This should have been devastating for all parties involved, but Grace and the author found it funny. Clothing went back on. Later that afternoon, Grace told me for the first time about her brother, who had committed suicide.

The Changs have a house in the woods, about three hours away from D.C. in West Virginia. They never go there. But they thought it was important to have a second house just to show that they were successful enough to have a second house. That makes them sound really shallow, which they aren't. Both of Grace's parents routinely save people's lives. The second house just shows that even really smart people can think stupid things.

The author and Grace will have sex in West Virginia some

day after college if it comes to that. If the world starts again.

Grace, Carlos, and Duck are the Neapolitans. That's the name Carlos came up with. He is chocolate smooth, Grace is strawberry sweet, and the author is pure vanilla.

Really though, Carlos is the looks, Grace the brains, and I'm supposed to be the funny one. Except Carlos is funnier than me. And not exactly a slouch when it comes to intellect either. Carlos is headed to Stanford. Grace is also funnier than me, but no one realizes that because she rarely lets her freak flag fly in public. I'm going to GW. My mom played the brain tumor card and got me in.

My mother didn't call me Duck. She hated that nickname.

Mackenzie Van de Kamp never called me Duck either—she calls me Duckie.

As in the character from *Pretty in Pink*. The one who is in love with the heroine but never gets her. Yeah, that's me. I've had a crush on Mackenzie since seventh grade when she decided to let me do her math homework for her. It's not like she couldn't do it herself; she just didn't want to. Carlos thought I was a putz for doing it, and he told Mackenzie that she could probably get a better grade if she did it herself. Mackenzie didn't really like Carlos since he is one of the few people who doesn't care what she thinks.

Mackenzie is rich. Most kids in LSGC(AWGWU) are, but Mackenzie has Serious Money, the kind that you could never spend no matter how hard you try. Her mother inherited a fortune and her father doubled it in real estate. They have a multi-million dollar house in Foxhall, but Mackenzie is often there alone because her parents are frequently in one of their other houses in other parts of the world, usually not together. Even if they are home, Mackenzie might not know it. She has her own wing. Seriously.

The author, on the other hand, shared a bathroom with both his parents since he was born. Until circumstances intervened and they were gone.

The author knows that he has been used by Mackenzie as a breakup buddy. He doesn't care. Every time Mackenzie broke up with a new guy, which was quite often, she invited the author over to her house to watch a double feature of her choosing. The first time, in eighth grade, it was *Pretty in Pink* (which led to the bastardization of his nickname) and *Silkwood*. It was always a disconcerting mix. Often it was also tailored to the boy she broke up with, with disturbing undertones. When she broke up with Patrick White, who was African-American, it was *Tales from the Hood* and *Do the Right Thing*. For Kanta Shizuki, who didn't really break up with her so much as get taken back to Japan with his diplomat parents, *Letters from Iwo Jima* and the Japanese version of *The Ring*. Jacob Schwartz: *Annie Hall* and *Schindler's List*.

As the credits rolled on the second movie, she would curl up in front of me on that giant couch in her private TV room, put my hand on her breast—always over the shirt—and start to move her hips against me until she felt me shudder. Then she'd kiss my hand and thank me and send me home on my bike or later in my car. Carlos told me I didn't need to do that, but he understood why I did. I never told Grace about those nights, but on some level she knew. Mackenzie always had a new boyfriend within two weeks.

Following My First Instinct,
Which Is a Crappy One

I HAVE ALREADY LIED to you, dear reader. I did know where I was going when I left my house the morning my mom died. I was headed to see Mackenzie. Horrible idea. But also completely predictable.

Running down Nebraska Avenue, I started to get winded. Man, was I out of shape. But every time I considered slowing down, I saw something new. A delivery man tossing a package into his truck—the box suspended in mid-air. A bird frozen in flight. Two overdressed women engaged in an eternal air kiss. Each image freaked me out more than the last. Better to run and let the world blur around me.

I slowed down to an awkward skip once I got off the main road into Mackenzie's neighborhood. I was too pumped up on adrenaline to just walk. That may have been the first time I thought it didn't matter if I looked like an idiot. No one would see me.

The houses in Foxhall are enormous and set back from the road. Everything is placid there. That is the way it is designed. No movement. Peace and quiet. Rich enough to buy distance from your neighbors. On those streets, I could almost convince myself nothing had changed.

Everything was going to be okay. Really, I believed that. Whatever was happening. Whatever episode I was having. Or whatever the world was churning through. It would all work itself out. I just needed to talk to Mackenzie.

When I saw her house, I started to run again, across the expansive lawn to the massive portico that sheltered the front door. My head began to clear. It was the middle of the afternoon. She wouldn't be home. Mackenzie had a job working for some senator as an intern for the summer. I decided it didn't matter. I'd be safe inside her house.

What I needed was to get into her bed and go to sleep and wait for it to pass. Mackenzie would come home after work and wake me. She'd be confused—what was I doing there? But she'd be happy to see me. And I'd tell her my fantastical tale. She'd laugh and call me crazy. *What a ridiculous dream*, she'd say. Then, I'd tell her my mom had died that morning. She'd pull me into her arms and cry with me and we'd cling to each other and fall asleep.

Yeah, whatever.

I tried the doorknob. Locked. Pressing my nose against the window, I looked into the entry hall, which was bigger than my living room. No one there. I rang the doorbell, hoping that their housekeeper or cook could let me in. But it didn't ring. No chimes. I tried a couple more times. Nothing. I made myself think that it was broken, knowing better.

Even rich people sometimes forget their keys. Around the side of the house, I scaled the fence and dropped into the backyard. It was a beautiful day for a swim, but the pool was almost always covered. The hot tub got a lot of use, but I didn't want to think about that. In the distance, I could see the tennis court where Mackenzie—in that too short skirt and too tight polo—tried to teach me to play. The key was stashed at the edge of patio, inside a statue by some famous modern sculptor.—

Mackenzie's mother had bought it for a boat load of money at auction. The price set some record for the guy. Mackenzie was impressed by it, but to me it looked like an oil drum with a propeller on top. It was hollow and perfect for hiding things. I reached inside, trying not to cut my hand on the rusty edges.

The key opened a back door into the rooms where the nanny/maid/cook used to live. Now they were guest rooms, I supposed. Or just dead space. In the house, I relaxed even more. Nothing should be moving here. No chance of an immobile car or bird or stray jogger. To get to Mackenzie's side of the house, I had to walk through the formal dining room and living room, past the den and the library, back into the entrance hall. I had already passed three bathrooms by the time I got to her room. Did I mention it was a big house?

Just get in her bed. Go to sleep. Wait for her to come home.

But when I got to the doorway of her bedroom, I saw Mackenzie. Naked. Perched on the edge of her bed. Face scrunched up in concentration in that adorable way of hers. In one hand, poised, a nail clipper. The other hand on her foot, picking up her big toe.

Naked. Why was she naked? Why was she here? She should be at work. But I knew. Mackenzie never cleaned up—they have a fleet of maids for that—so it was not surprising to find her clothes strewn about. Bras, thongs, skimpy tops—I used to suspect that she threw them on the floor just to tease me when I came over, so it was somewhat comforting to see that those things were always on the floor.

His clothes were there too. A suit jacket and pants draped over her desk chair. The dress shirt, tie and belt mingling with Mackenzie's things on the floor. I had never seen Mackenzie naked before. This should have been a transcendent moment. But all I could think was, *Where the hell is he?*

Last night, when things still moved and my mother lay in her hospital bed on the first floor rasping out her last breaths, I checked Facebook. I could barely see the screen through the tears, but at that point I was desperate for a distraction. It didn't really work, but I remembered Mackenzie's post. *Tomorrow, Brookings event with LD.* LD: Legislative Director.

I checked the closet, figuring that they had heard me come in and he was hiding. But that was logic from my previous world. No one there, of course. "Where the hell is he?" I yelled. Mackenzie's focus on her cuticle was Zen-like. She had reached satori—the entire world had—except for me.

He's in the shower, I thought.

No, I don't hear any water.

You're a complete idiot who has not wrapped your brain around the unusual but undeniable circumstances in which you find yourself.

Then I knew. *He's in the shower.*

I found him holding her shampoo bottle, lathered suds in his hair. A smile on his lips, post-sex, warm water on his back, limp penis pointing south. A ring on his finger—married. But he was younger than I expected—maybe late twenties or early thirties—given that he was running legislative policy for a senator, but then that's how the Hill works. They like 'em young.

I wondered if there was even a Brookings event to attend. Or was that just a cover to let them get away for a couple of hours. Mackenzie had been working in the office for less than a week. That was fast even for her.

Now seems like a good place to explain what people feel like in the frozen world. Skin feels like skin, hair like hair, lips like lips. It's one of those things that is almost normal. When no one moves, you expect them to feel like molded plastic, like mannequins, limbs swiveling on set pivots without much range. A secondary possibility was that everyone would feel rubbery, like the well-preserved fetal pig Grace dissected for me. Wrong on both counts.

The inert water hung down from the showerhead like strands of silk caressing his body. I touched one and it came away from its cohorts, wet and liquid on my fingertips.

It had been almost a month since prom. Mackenzie's boyfriend of the moment had dumped her the afternoon of the dance. She had called me as I was putting on my tuxedo and asked me to come over, to spend the night with her instead. I could hear her crying as she told me it would be worth my while. That we had so much history, but so much more to come. She would be going to Harvard in the fall—all the Van de Kamps go to Harvard—we had a whole summer to be together and figure out what we had. But it turned out to be just another typical breakup night. We watched *Carrie* and *Footloose*.

I drove home around two in the morning with wet boxers. The night hospice nurse was dozing in the chair near my mom's hospital bed in what used to be our living room. I hadn't seen Mackenzie since.

I stared at the naked married guy in her shower. He had that frat boy jock look about him, though he was starting to get flab where once he had muscle. I imagined there was a cute perky wife out there who had come to D.C. with him as he followed the power of his newly elected senator. They were going to take the world by storm but now she was probably starting to sag too. I wondered if she knew he was cheating on her with an eighteen-year-old. Still, it didn't really matter because they were both frozen, like the rest of them.

I took some suds from his hair and rubbed them in his eyes. I turned the water all the way to hot. Flush with victory, I gathered up his suit and tie and underwear and shoes and everything of his I could find and tossed them into the shower with him.

Vaguely satisfied, I went and sat next to Mackenzie. I wanted to say something gracious about how wonderful our time had been together, how much I would love her forever, but that we couldn't go on like this. I intended to kiss her gently on the lips and say goodbye. But her nakedness mocked me. Like a river trawler, I scooped up as much of her clothing off the floor and threw it over her head, so it fluttered down around her. I might have let out a grunt. As a show of anger, it was pretty pathetic. Was I really breaking up with someone I wasn't dating? She was still naked, but now with a blouse over her head like a burka and a thong hanging off the nail clipper in her hand. I started to hyperventilate. I had to get out of there.

Halfway to the door, I decided to steal Mackenzie's car. Through the kitchen and the laundry room and the back den and the mud room was the four-car garage. I really had spent way too much time in this house. Her car was the cobalt-blue Beemer—one of the few things I knew for a fact that she loved. The keys were hanging on a hook by the door. The fob shook in my hand as I clicked the button to unlock the car.

Nothing happened. The lights didn't blink. The horn didn't chirp. No sign that the car had unlocked. Sure enough, the door wouldn't open when I pulled the handle. That was Mackenzie for you—lock the car door, then leave the key in plain sight. So I opened it the old fashioned way, with the key in the lock. How quaint.

Sitting in the driver's seat, enveloped in the smell of her perfume, I jabbed at the garage door button. Again, nothing. I poked it again and again. Nada. Already knowing the result, I put the key in the ignition and turned. The engine wouldn't turn over. Not even a sputter. So much for stealing a car.

Mackenzie's dad is some sort of biking enthusiast. When he wasn't working—he worked almost all the time—he would go on these massively long rides all over the region. There were ten bikes hanging on the wall, each one a fancier racing model than the last. Resigned to more exercise, I squeezed all twenty tires and took the bike with the most air. I wheeled it through the house and out the front door.

Outside, nothing had changed. Still beautiful. Still sunny. Still seventy-one degrees. Still frozen.

Discussion: Machines

IN YOUR FROZEN WORLD, you will be most frustrated by the fact that the machines have stopped working. It is the polar opposite of the Terminator apocalypse. Anything that runs on electricity is dead. Anything that needs a battery. Motors that require a spark to start. Not broken—dead. I'm sure that the machines that worked at this moment will work during the next, if it ever comes. But in the frozen world they are all useless. No cars to drive. No TVs to watch.

You will have an overwhelming urge to surf the web for an answer. Maybe to check the warranty manual. You can't.

Electrical impulses no longer travel through the wires—they are stuck exactly where they were at that moment. Lights are either on or off, and there ain't a damn thing to do about it. Wireless signals hang uselessly in the air around you. Waving your phone around to try and catch them won't work. Trust me. Your iPhone is a coaster.

Other simpler devices have also been rendered impotent. Striking a match merely leaves a smudge of phosphorous. If you need a spark, you're out of luck.

There are machines that work. You can peddle a bicycle. You

can hit the keys on a typewriter—manual, not electric—and it will strike the paper. If you find a radio with a crank on it, you could give it a little juice, but don't expect to find a radio station. You could also probably make a perfectly fine lever or pulley. Knock yourself out.

Luckily for the author, he had already disconnected himself from most of the modern world in the months leading up to the end.

I was down to checking Facebook only a couple of times a day. Never used my Twitter or Instagram or Tumblr accounts anymore. YouTube videos could barely hold my attention. I had a complete lack of Pinterest. I hadn't turned on the TV in weeks. I mainly read books. Those still work. The real ones, with paper pages. Your Kindle might as well be a slab of granite for all the good it'll do you.

Seriously, What the Hell Happened?

I HAVE SOME POSSIBLE theories:

#1: God hates me.

That was a lousy place to start. Where the hell do you go from there? Am I being punished? For what? I am Adam cast out of the Garden. I am Jonah in the whale. (See? I did learn something in my tenth-grade Bible as Literature class—thanks, Mrs. K!) But that premise suggests that I have to do something to get back into God's good graces. Which would lead to a sub-theory.

#1a: God wants me to repent.

Can't figure out what for. Doesn't help. Moving on.

#2: God has forsaken us.

This one takes the blame off my shoulders, but is not exactly comforting. Kind of like God is a little kid and the Earth a forgotten toy that rolled under the bed where the battery slowly ran down. There's just enough power left to keep me going. And nothing is going to change until God cleans his room and finds us and recharges the world, or at least sells Earth at a garage sale to let some other God play with us for a while.

#3: The aliens are coming.

There are a number of ways this one goes. The aliens are coming to kill us all, but first they froze the world with a giant freezing ray so they can take over without worrying about anything but incinerating a bunch of immobile life forms. But they didn't count on one man being immune to the effects of the ray. And that one hero—me—will vanquish them and bring back humanity. This is the Hollywood screenplay. One problem—no sign of aliens. That leads to …

#3a: I am the aliens' guinea pig.

The aforementioned aliens have set this all up as an experiment to study me to see how I'll react under extreme circumstances.

I'm the rat running through the maze. No thank you.

#4: I'm stuck in the Matrix.

In this one, none of this is real. I'm Keanu Reeves stuck in my little water cocoon with wires plugged into the back of my head feeding me an entire virtual reality. But there is a malfunction in the computer program, and I'm the only one getting any input. That would explain why everyone else is stuck. A computer glitch. We need to reboot. Big problem: I don't look anything like Keanu Reeves.

#4a: A government experiment has gone awry.

Somewhere in a bunker the poor schmucks who designed the time-stopping machine are frozen just like everyone else. Or maybe they're watching me navigate through it, unable to leave their bunker without being affected themselves. Which would be similar to #3a, except my adversary in the movie would be Donald Sutherland in a military uniform rather than Andy Serkis in a motion capture suit.

#5: I'm crazy.

I'm sitting in a rubber room in an institution somewhere, being force-fed medications that keep me docile. This world is all in my head. This theory scares me, so I don't think about it, even though it is pretty solid, given my family history.

#6: There is no logic in the universe.

This is all random, and the universe is unexplainable. I have no control over my fate or the events of this world.

Yeah, that's the one I really don't like. The one that makes my throat constrict. I don't like to think about it all having no meaning whatsoever. There has to be a reason.

I'm 17. What Do You Expect?

THE BIKE WAS A great idea. I flew down Massachusetts Avenue, past the giant embassy buildings. The faster I went the more it seemed like the world was back in motion. I'd catch things in my peripheral vision as I passed, and they seemed mobile. Everything was a blur and that was perfect.

All those diplomats behind their iron fences. I wondered if the entire world was frozen. It had to be. Or would a fleet of Russian or French helicopters come storming over the horizon at any moment to rescue me? I'm pretty weak at learning foreign languages, so I hoped it wouldn't come to that. Carlos was spending the summer in some South American country— Bolivia or maybe Paraguay—digging wells or assisting at a rural clinic or something, generally doing good and shoring up his credentials for when he inevitably runs for the senate. From here, I could easily get to Georgetown, but he wouldn't be there. So I just coasted and tried not to think much about where I was going.

The frozen world leads naturally to digressions. Your brain has ample time to wander, which is ironic given that time is not something available to anyone else. You've got the market cornered.

I started thinking about superpowers. Like every kid, I'd always dreamed of being a superhero. In my unhappiest moments, I would think that maybe I just had to reach my lowest point, rock bottom, and then the aliens or the supreme beings or the imperial council of the universe or whoever it was that had the means to distribute superpowers would appear and say, you have been chosen, having passed the trials and tribulations required of a champion to receive the power of whatever. The power was different every time. I vacillated between which superhuman ability would be the best.

Flying was always a possibility. Soaring over the city, spotting criminals and ne'er-do-wells. And then what? Call the police? The problem with flight was that it really had to be combined with another superpower to be at all useful. Maybe super-strength, so you could take girls for rides. I was reasonably sure that if all I had was flight I would never help anyone. I can probably lift about fifty pounds for an extended period, which would barely allow me to save a child from a burning building, let alone take some hot chick on a tour of the city. Besides, I was convinced that I would be able to fly, but I wouldn't be able to control the flight. I figured I would know how to take off, but not land or slow down or turn. So, I might rocket right into space and be unable to breathe, probably dying just as the pressure of the vacuum made my head explode due to the distinct lack of the necessary complementary superpower. Or I might take off and coast along perfectly fine for a while until I hit a building or got tangled up in some power lines.

This happened with every superpower I fantasized about having. I uncovered the reasons it wouldn't be that super, and then because that wasn't negative enough, I moved on to the various ways each particular superpower might actually kill me.

Teleportation. How would I know where I would end

up? Maybe stuck halfway through a block of concrete. Or a thousand feet below the surface of the ocean. Or into the direct line of gunfire in a drug-gang shootout. There was an endless array of places where a person would not want to appear unprepared.

Superstrength. I wouldn't be able to regulate the pressure and thus would break everything I touched. The sidewalk would crack beneath my feet. Buildings would crumble at the touch of my fingertips. I would be cast out to live in the desert. A pariah.

Superspeed. See Flying.

Hearing people's thoughts. I would learn exactly what everyone thought about me and would be so devastated that I would just curl up into a fetal position and never leave the house again. The cacophony of thoughts wouldn't end and I would go mad.

And so on and so on and so on. Heat vision burned my retinas, causing me to go blind. Superhearing gave me splitting headaches. Elasticity broke all my bones. Telekinesis resulted in me getting crushed by a piano.

Invisibility. It always came down to invisibility. Sure, there were problems with that too. I could get hurt and no one would be able to find me and take me to the hospital. I could get run over by a car whose driver never saw me. But all of that was manageable. After all, I could get run down by a car right now. And the benefits greatly outweighed the risks. Invisibility was an all-access backstage pass to houses, bathrooms, locker rooms, dressing rooms.

Dorms.

I had pedaled onto the George Washington campus on autopilot. I found myself coasting past the library where my mom worked. I wondered if they would name something after her, maybe a room or a hallway.

Shoving that aside, I thought about Mackenzie and her married lover. That fueled the anger and helped me justify where I'd been headed all along. To use my superpower. In the frozen world, I was already invisible.

I was looking for naked girls.

Fine, I said it. Not proud. But that's what I was doing. Sorry, Mom.

There are a bunch of dorms at GW clustered together in Foggy Bottom. There is always someone coming and someone going, so I was allowed access to nearly all the buildings despite the fact that none of the electronic buzzer locks would work. I visited floor by floor, methodically checking doorknobs, going into the bathrooms. It is amazing how many college students shower at 1:17 p.m. Thirty-seven co-eds at various stages of undress. I must admit that, while it was the pure manifestation of my fourteen-year-old kid invisible man fantasy, the actuality of it became quite clinical, even non-sexual, after a bit. While I have told you that people do not feel any different to the touch, they surely look different in this frozen world, particularly bodies that should be, but are not, in motion. Bear with me, but this is particularly true of uncovered breasts.

These girls in these showers, going about their basic routine—soaping up, washing hair, shaving legs—were in constant motion. But to see them frozen at a particular moment meant that many of their breasts appeared to be suspended by strings, hanging unnaturally where they should be falling back to their usual position. And I found myself noticing the irregularities—indentations where fingers had just brushed them, lift where there should be sag.

Each time I found a girl, I wanted to feel like I was getting back at Mackenzie for her many transgressions. All of her relationships that weren't with me. Instead I found myself thinking that I would be at school here with all these girls next year. Maybe one would be my TA or RA. Maybe we'd have a class together and end up in a study group. I'd surely remember them and be nervous and they wouldn't know why, but then again I'm going to be nervous around everyone so they probably won't notice anyway. Some of them were pretty attractive, the kind of girls I'd want to hook up with. If I was the last man on Earth, which I am, would you sleep with me?

But the thoughts always circled around to the same end. I'm never going to college because the world is frozen. I'm never even going to be eighteen.

Doors to the dorm rooms themselves were generally locked. Sometimes I would find a student on the way in or out, but that usually meant the room itself was empty or occupied by a fully clothed roommate. Other times, I would snag a key from a girl in the stairwell and try each door on the adjoining floor, hoping to catch a roommate who knew she had some free moments alone.

I was only successful once. The girl was only a few paces away from her door when I snatched her keys. A suite. In one of the bedrooms, a naked guy was looming at the height of a pushup over a naked girl who lay flat on her back on the bed. They must have started before the roommate left. They were on top of the covers, in full view of the invisible man. Her left breast spilled over her side. But her right was pointing straight up, almost like a teepee. It took a while for me to process that she must have been shifting her weight at exactly that moment, rolling just a bit, adjusting. The couple looked like an illustration from an anatomy textbook: here's how you make a baby, step one.

I sat down in the chair at her desk and stared at them for a while. He looked intent, determined. But it was her expression that bothered me. Was that concern in her eyes, apprehension? Fear?

If you look at anything long enough, you can convince yourself that you are seeing exactly what you have just convinced yourself you are seeing. Was he holding her down? His hands were on her arms. Was she too drunk or high to say no? I got real close to her face, trying to ferret out bloodshot in her eyes. Had she been drugged?

Was he raping her? Was that twisting of her body a last-minute attempt to get away? Did she need help?

I don't know how long I had been there when I decided I needed to stop this. He was precariously perched, easily tipped off the bed. He landed hard on the floor, rolled over on his side, his penis touching the ground like the third leg of a tripod.

The Invisible Man saves the day. And what thanks did I get? The girl stared at the ceiling, same expression as before, still completely unreadable. But without the guy in the way, her body language was now unmistakable. Ready, waiting, wanting to have sex.

My father, the philosopher, once wrote that there is no good or evil without time. Empirically, he argued, man's actions in themselves are not right or wrong. It is only the interaction of those deeds with the passage of time and the judgments of others that leads to morality. If you were to freeze time at the instant of the act, and never allow for there to be recriminations or regret or accusations or revenge, then the act itself becomes a meaningless one. No matter what that act is. Merely a moment detached from all other moments. A moment without consequence.

This was the moment when I fully understood that not only might I lose my mind, but also my soul. The temptation before me was great. I am the superman. I am the one and only God. In this world, I am a deity. And everything that happens is due to my will. Everything that happens is by my hand.

This girl is mine. She belongs to me.

I could have her.

A moment with no consequence.

I didn't do it. Walking out of that room with an unresolved erection, imagining myself screwing the girl with the spread legs and worried eyes, I knew without a doubt that my father was wrong.

I needed to talk to someone. There was no one.

I needed to find Grace.

Discussion: Sex

You may be wondering if sex is the same in the frozen world. How the hell would I know? I'm a virgin.

The author can safely say, as has already been expressed, that thinking about sex has not changed. It is a constant and it is unfortunate.

Come to think of it, sex is probably illegal in the frozen world. Because unless there is more than one of you moving, any partner you manage to find is by definition going to be non-consenting.

For the record, masturbation is pretty much the same.

The Day Time Should Have Stopped

IT WAS JUST ABOUT seven months ago that my mother was diagnosed. It was a day a lot like today. Sunny, warm, probably seventy-one degrees. I think there were five of us sitting on the steps outside of the GW student center. Me, Carlos, and Grace. And Lindsey Andreotti and Liz Richardson. We called them the Olsen twins because they were blonde and skinny, looked a bit vacant, and were always together. They were pretty smart though, like everyone at LSGC(AWGWU). We were all getting credit for taking a GW freshman calculus class. One of the perks of LSGC(AWGWU) was that the college curriculum was open to us as high school students in certain circumstances. It wasn't that the classes were so fun, but hanging out on campus and pretending that we were cooler than we were … that was fun. That's what we were doing.

I guess it was six of us when Mackenzie wandered out of the building—she had been flirting with our TA—and asked Carlos for a cigarette. Carlos didn't smoke much, but he always had a pack on him to give one to the girls. Lindsey and Liz already had cigs hanging at identical angles out of their mouths. Carlos lit one for Mackenzie.

I don't smoke. Tried it once. Nearly passed out from the hacking. Grace never tried it. Child of two surgeons and all. Actually, that was the last time I remember Carlos having cigarettes on him. He tossed them when my mom got cancer.

"We should go to a bar," Mackenzie said, taking a deep drag and blowing smoke out of the side of her mouth. It was 3:30 in the afternoon.

Lindsey and Liz nodded in unison. I actually liked both of them. They were good to talk to if you could separate them from each other. But together it was like communicating with the Borg. Yeah, I'm a nerd.

Mackenzie was looking at Carlos. She knew that he was the only one who could make her off-hand request happen. He made a lot of things happen. Somehow when he was with her, the bartenders never questioned her fake ID. There was a bar nearby on Pennsylvania that was particularly lax.

"I've got to get home and change. Award ceremony tonight."

I knew it wasn't an award for him. Must be for his mom or dad. Or maybe one of his sisters. No one questioned that a Delgado would be getting an award. Pretty routine.

Mackenzie puffed some smoke out of her nose in defeat and dropped in between me and Carlos on the stairs. I could feel Grace tense up behind me. But none of that really mattered. I was just warm and happy. Watching the college kids walk by. Having nowhere to go, nothing to do. It was the first time that day that I had forgotten about my mom's appointment.

She'd been complaining about feeling off. A bit woozy, with occasional blurred vision. Sometimes she'd stand up and have to sit right back down. All she would say to me was that her leg must have fallen asleep. But it wasn't until the headaches that she finally made an appointment, which led to some tests, which led to the appointment she was having today. It's just migraines, she said. I tried to believe her.

"We'll go with you," Lindsey said.

Mackenzie didn't turn around, though it was obvious Lindsey was talking to her.

Liz piped in. "Yeah, I could use a drink."

Mackenzie heaved a deep sigh. I was familiar with that noise, the sound of her pretending she was about to do something she didn't want to. "Fine. In a few. I want to bask."

She tipped her head back and closed her eyes, fully aware that arching her back strained her breasts against her blouse. Carlos and I both smiled as we caught the other staring.

My cell rang. It was Mom.

When she heard my phone, Mackenzie leaned my way, nudging her head against my arm, her hair falling into my lap. I've known Mackenzie long enough to realize she didn't want me to answer a call when I could be paying attention to her. Grace nudged my shoulder; she knew who it was.

"You've got to answer," she said.

Her voice snapped me out of my reverie. I stood up and Mackenzie pretended to fall over a bit. Righting herself, she puffed out her disapproval again. I walked a couple of steps away down the sidewalk before answering.

"Hey, Mom. What's up?"

It sounded like she started to say something, but all I heard was her sucking in air quickly on the other side. The words caught in her throat.

"Mom?"

"I ... I need you to come get me."

"Didn't you drive?"

"I ... I can't."

"What did the doctor say?"

She didn't answer.

"Mom?"

"Are you her son?" Another voice on the line.

"Who is this? Where is my mom?"

"She's still here in the office. You need to come pick her up."

The voice never did identify itself. A nurse or a receptionist. It didn't matter. I'd stopped processing anything. GW Hospital was right around the corner. The voice told me which room to go to. I repeated it out loud. Only then did I realize that Grace was standing next to me. I hung up my phone.

"What'd she say?" Grace said.

"Nothing. She could barely talk."

Mackenzie was standing with the Olsen twins, getting ready to leave. Carlos was on the curb, hand out for a cab. I wandered in their direction.

"Last chance to join three hot chicks at the bar," Mackenzie said, sort of to Carlos, sort of to me.

Carlos ignored her. "What's up, Duck?"

I remembered when his saying that used to get a laugh. He'd make a half effort at a Bugs Bunny impression and fail, which somehow made the girls laugh harder. So long ago.

"I think something's wrong. I gotta get my mom."

I don't know why I did it, but I looked right at Mackenzie when I said it. I do know why. I wanted her to go with me. After everything, I went to her first.

"So that's a no on the bar then," Mackenzie said.

She stared me down. *You can't make me care.*

"Yeah," Grace said, with every ounce of sarcasm she had. "No bar."

"Catch you later then."

Mackenzie turned and walked away, followed closely by the Olsens. So cold, yet I found myself already forgiving her.

Carlos waited a moment. "You want company?"

"It's probably nothing. You've got your thing. Maybe they just gave her some drugs for another test and she forgot to tell me."

But I knew that there were no tests scheduled for today.

"I'll go," Grace said.

"Okay, but hit me if you need anything, got it?"

I nodded. Carlos stuck his hand back out and a cab magically pulled up in front of him.

Grace and I must have walked the few blocks to the hospital, then gone into the building and up an escalator. I don't remember.

My mom was sitting in the waiting room in a chair in the corner. She looked tiny, like she could disappear. There was an unopened magazine on her lap. She was staring at the pattern on the wallpaper, flowers and leaves.

I sat down next to her. Grace walked up to the receptionist, leaving us alone.

"Mom? What happened?"

She turned. Her eyes seemed unfocused, looking right through me.

"Hey, kiddo. How was class?"

Her voice was drained of life. Her lips trembled slightly.

"Fine. You okay?"

That was when she took my hand. I couldn't remember the last time that we had held hands, probably not since I was in elementary school. Her palm was clammy, her fingers cold. All the conviction that was absent from her voice was in her grip. Now I was scared.

"Tumor."

She barely whispered the world. Then, she turned back to the wallpaper.

"Duck, the doctor wants to talk to you," Grace said.

I don't know how much time passed between my mother's last word and Grace's reappearance. There are moments that last forever. When nothing moves. All goes quiet. Everything would be different if time had really stopped before my mom said that word.

But it didn't. It waited seven months, long after everything went to hell.

Then, there was a doctor kneeling in front of us. He looked impossibly young. My vision was clouding over, but I wasn't going to cry. The words came out in snippets. Glioblastoma. Surgery. Chemo. Aggressive. Later, when I needed to remember, Grace repeated the doctor's speech back to me verbatim.

I probably shouldn't have driven us home, but I insisted. I needed to anchor myself to the wheel. I needed to take control.

My mom in the passenger seat, Grace in the back. No one said anything until we got close to Grace's house.

"We need to drop Grace off," my mom said.

"It's okay. I'll take the metro back."

"That's silly. We're right here."

She nodded to me and I could see my mother emerging from the depths. Maybe this would be okay. I pulled off Connecticut at Woodley and wove through the neighborhood, pulling up in front of Grace's house.

"Call me if you need anything," Grace said. She gave my shoulder a squeeze.

My mom answered. "Thanks, Grace. You're a dear." A pause, and when I saw her smirk I knew my mother was back, at least for a while. "But you know I hate it when you call him Duck."

Mise-en-scène: Smithsonian Natural History Museum

I WAS PRETTY WORKED up by the time I got to the museum. It was farther from GW than I remembered. Even pedaling non-stop, skidding my way around the corners, weaving in and out of the motionless cars, trying not to hit any pedestrians, I felt like I was moving impossibly slow, like I was running out of charge and winding down to a stop. It wasn't true, of course. I was flying. Dangerously so. Reckless. I could have easily brained myself on a tree or monument. But I made it.

There was a line out the front door at Natural History. There usually is. Things get backed up at the metal detector as the guards rummage through bags. I hopped off my bike without stopping and let it roll away from me into a jersey barrier. Admired it as it went. It was nice to see something else move on its own.

But I had no time for nostalgia. I had a goal. Find Grace. She was somewhere in the massive building before me. Before I could stop myself with logic—such as the fact that I had no idea where anything was in this massive building or that I wasn't even really sure that Grace worked here—I bounded up the stairs past the line and inside.

I had started to get used to the frozen people, but I had never been quite so surrounded by them. The atrium was packed. I went through the metal detector—on the off chance that I might set it off and wake up the world—then into the fray. It was hard to walk in any direction without bumping someone. Tour groups clustered together, taking up large chunks of real estate: Japanese tourists following a yellow flag, elementary school crossing guards wearing bright orange belts, a church group proudly sporting Jesus on their t-shirts. In between them were the families trailing toddlers and pushing strollers, the couples whose clasped hands created additional barriers, the singletons who were gazing earnestly around the room searching for their companions. Their collective inactivity had a movement of its own. So much potential that I could almost fool myself into thinking they were moving beyond my peripheral vision. Not true, of course.

At the center of the atrium was the elephant. Proudly raising its trunk above the crowd. Stuffed. Not supposed to move. I stared at it for a moment, wondering if freezing the world would lead to the static exhibits coming to life. My mom loved *Night at the Museum*—particularly Attila the Hun. His rebirth would have been a nice tribute to her, but the elephant remained stoic and still.

So there I was. Where to start looking for Grace? Not in the main exhibits, certainly. She'd be somewhere behind the scenes. In the guts of the massive building, which really is massive.

To my left was the mammals exhibit, to my right the dinosaurs. Ahead, sea life. I looked up at the elephant again. This whole place was full of dead things. I took a deep breath and reminded myself that those are different than the living statues around me. Even though they aren't moving. Even though they aren't breathing.

Command decision time. I chose mammals. Somehow that felt less threatening than the extinct prehistoric lizards or the vast expanse of the ocean. Really, I wasn't there to browse and learn. I needed to find a door marked STAFF ONLY.

I hadn't talked to Grace in three days. That was the longest period of time I had not had contact with her since we met. Carlos and me, we'd sometimes go days without talking, though with texts and Snapchat smack flying constantly. With Grace there was never a day where we didn't call each other. Even when she took that trip to Taiwan, there was Skype.

I was honestly not sure if she stopped talking to me or I stopped talking to her. We just stopped. We both had reasons. I did stand her up for the prom when I went over to Mackenzie's. That sucked. But that probably wasn't it. It wasn't really a date. I skipped graduation and she was mad that I missed her party. Or maybe it was because I blamed her parents for letting my mom die. Yeah, that's probably it.

See, here's the thing. I didn't want my mom to die. It's that simple, really. What isn't so simple is that Grace's parents are both doctors. To be honest, I don't know what kind of surgeons they are. I guess I should have asked that before I asked Grace to have them consult with my mom's doctors about her condition. But all I knew was that they were both based at GW and I didn't know whether I could trust anyone and my mom was getting worse and what the fuck did I know about anything and I needed someone to tell me that we were doing what we needed to do.

So they checked on her and talked to all her doctors. Grace invited me over for dinner. I knew it was bad when both Mr. and Mrs.—or I should say Dr. and Dr.?—Chang were there. They were never both home at the same time. Never. And Grace's sister had been shipped out to a friend's for a sleepover. They felt they needed some time alone with me.

They told me everything I knew. The tumor was growing. The treatment hadn't worked. The cancer was terminal. It was just a matter of time.

They said other things. We will continue to help out at the

hospital. We will always be here for you. You are not alone.

Grace said nothing. I said nothing. I didn't cry. No one hugged. I went home. Sat down next to my mom's hospital bed in the living room, watched her sleep, and thought about how long she had left. That was when she was still lucid. She was weakening but not bedridden. It was one of the last days I could pretend it would be okay.

The next morning, I realized that I hated Grace's parents for letting me down. I believed that they would fix her. Not logically, not in my head, but in the small deeply hidden part of my soul where I was still a lonely child.

Three days ago—give or take whatever amount of undetermined time that the world has been frozen—I told Grace how I felt. She didn't react well.

"They didn't want to get involved," she said. "I made them do it. You needed to hear it. You're so damn selfish. I told you I needed you to be at my graduation party. I told you that. And you weren't there. I needed you."

It all spilled out of her in a flurry, without a breath, so fast that it took a moment for me to realize she had changed subjects midstream. It would have probably been fine if we had been together, but we were on the phone.

"I'm selfish?"

It was a question, but I was so angry it sounded more like a threat. Although in Grace's defense, looking back, I was selfish. But if you can't be selfish when your mother is dying, when can you be?

"Yes. Selfish. You're going to have to move on."

Move on? My mother wasn't dead yet. Move on?

"I know she's going to die. Your parents killed her."

I think that is pretty much a direct quote. It didn't even make sense. But I said it with conviction. Silence at the other end of the line. It took me a few minutes to realize that Grace had hung up.

Walking among the mammals, stuffed and arranged around

the cavernous room in poses meant to evoke the illusion of life, I wished that I had been less selfish. My anger pre-death was all sadness post. Grace needed me at her graduation party. I had no idea why and I hadn't asked. Now, all I wanted to do was find her and apologize.

The first staff door I found was locked. There was an electronic keypad, which I knew wouldn't work in the frozen world. I walked around the periphery of the exhibit. The animals were grouped by regions—South America, Australia, Asia. Somewhere between the Arctic and Europe, there was another door tucked into a corner. A scruffy looking guy with a badge was half in, half out, holding the door open.

Scruffy Dude kind of sneered at me as I realized he was blocking the door just enough to keep me from getting through without touching him. I gave the guy a little nudge. He started to sway, like a small tree in a stiff breeze.

Then, he started to fall backward.

Oh, crap.

I lunged for him. Last thing I needed on my conscience was some government type cracking his head on the industrial concrete floor of the Smithsonian. Probably a federal offense. True, I'd never know if he felt it, and he probably wouldn't either, but I didn't have time to think that through. He was picking up speed. I got my arms around his waist, but that was a mistake because his terminal velocity pulled us both to the ground. We sprawled back into the restricted area, his full weight coming down on my arm behind him, driving my elbow into the aforementioned industrial concrete.

Mother-loving son of a beast (or some similar combination)! That hurt.

Cradling my arm and clenching my teeth against the stinging pain, I watched the door close. Slowly, deliberately, until it latched shut. We had knocked against it as we fell, providing the inertia that allowed it to continue its motion to a conclusive click of its locking mechanism.

The Smithsonian guy lay still on the floor in front of me, his hand stretched out in front of him, reaching for the door handle. He looked a little desperate to grab it. His expression really was hard to read. But mostly he—more than anyone else I'd seen since the world ended—reminded me of a corpse in full-on rigor mortis.

Somewhere my mother was lying in the back of a hearse.

I sat there for a while, staring at him. Not thinking about much. Thinking about everything. The hallway was blindingly white and the door had no windows. I felt like I had fallen into a psych ward and was just waiting for the beefy orderlies to find us and return us to our padded cells. I was hungry. I was tired. I was a bit nauseous. I was alone. A dangerous spiral of a sudden reverie. For a moment, I believed I could sit there forever. Waiting.

The door was locked. I knew it when I heard the click. But I got to my feet anyway to check. Yup. Locked. There was a grayish pad on the wall. If I had touched the guy's badge to it and electrical impulses still worked, the door would have opened.

But they don't and it didn't. I was locked in.

Now I was scared.

After all, I hadn't locked myself in the cafeteria. This was more like a tomb. I ran down the sterile hallway and found another passage that looked much the same. There were doors, all of them locked. Peering through windows, I found desks and papers piled high, books and computers, each one looking more like an office of a liberal arts professor than the last. Some of the desks had more interesting objects among the mundane—a colorful bowl decorated with animals, the bones of a large creature, dozens of abalone shells, a primitive statue that appeared to have both breasts and a startlingly erect penis. But I didn't linger for long at any of the windows. I rattled the handle with my sweaty hand and moved on.

I found a staircase and decided to go down. There I found

more hallways, each as barren as the last. More doors locked. Here I was denied access to enormous storage rooms filled with wonders that for one reason or another were left off display. Shelves stretched away from me, loaded down with ancient artifacts of distant peoples, like the cluttered garage of ancient man. Another window, another darkened room, but here row after row of jars filled with milky liquids and in each the hint of an outline of a beak or a tentacle or a fin. In another, there were no shelves, just large animals loitering—a horse, a rhino, an okapi—close enough to each other to give the impression that they were a very odd herd, or possibly three strangers waiting for a bus. Maybe they were there for repairs—giant stuffed animals that had been loved a little too much and were now bleeding stuffing from their stomachs.

I moved on. I don't know how long I searched. Looking through windows, trying doors. Every exit was locked. That had to be fire hazard. I went upstairs and downstairs until I had no idea what floor I was on. My fear gave way to a conviction that this was where I would starve to death.

The doors all had identifying signs next to them. But they were indecipherable to me. Random strings of numbers and letters. B6-432. 1A-F3S. RQ-11. There didn't seem to be any logic. It was all designed to confuse me.

Occasionally, I came across a room where someone had taped up a handwritten or printed sign. Some were helpful: "PALEONTOLOGY—LARGE MAMMALS" or "INSTRUMENTS IN USE—KNOCK LOUDLY." Others were whimsical: "BONES" or "COSTUMES" or "HORNS."

Mollusks.

That one was handwritten. I recognized the sloping M and the rounded esses.

Grace.

But when I pressed my nose against the glass—yes, like a street urchin at a bakery in a Dickens novel—I didn't find my friend. There were two people in the room. An older man with an impressive salt-and-pepper beard and a younger woman with glasses and a blonde ponytail. The man was holding up two conch shells, presenting them for the consideration of the woman, who stared intently at the one on the left. She could have been an intern—she was younger than I thought when I first saw her. This could have been a test. Then I noticed that they each had food in front of them. This could also be lunchtime entertainment.

There was a third chair at the table, which I suspected was often used for performing dissections in addition to enjoying lively meals, and in front of it was a bowl of soup and a salad. I pressed my face harder into the glass, trying to see every inch of the room, searching for the third person. But I couldn't see anyone.

That was when I realized that I would never find Grace. That could be her lunch, but she was not there. She could be anywhere.

I wanted to escape. I wanted to eat that food. I wanted the weirdo with the conch to show them to me and ask me the riddle that the ponytail girl was so engrossed in solving. I wanted to talk to Grace.

I knew I wasn't going to get anything I wanted.

I stopped looking in the windows. Time to focus on getting out of the bowels of this museum. Door after door was locked, but finally, up two more flights, I found another door held ajar by another Smithsonian staffer, and this time I didn't mind sending him tumbling to the ground as I burst back out into the museum space.

Tourists again. Fewer than in the main hall, but enough to make me feel that I had returned to the real world, frozen though it was.

I sat on the floor for a while, and if I were the type of person who cried when he is relieved, I would have cried. I'm the type of person who stares blankly at the wall, so I did that instead.

Except it wasn't a wall. It was a giant geode. The crystals

inside it didn't sparkle. Not exactly. They were mid-sparkle, unchanging, but still bright. I stared into it, through it, and recovered.

A young girl was also fascinated by the geode, standing on her tiptoes and leaning against a railing so that she could get a better look inside. I don't know much about kids, but since this girl wasn't in school, I figured maybe she was four or five. Old enough to wander without constant supervision. But not too far. There was a woman sitting on a bench nearby next to a younger boy who was in the middle of a serious crying fit. The boy and girl were clearly siblings. The mother looked exhausted, eyes half-closed, mid-sigh, gathering strength to re-engage with her angry son. Not paying attention to her inquisitive daughter.

I know I'm not being fair to her. Probably this moment was misleading. It could be that she had been glancing at the girl while dealing with the boy. I stood up and walked over to the bench. The boy's mouth was open wide, tears on his cheeks, snot dripping from his nose. The noise from his wailing must have echoed impressively in the quiet museum. Others around the room were looking in his direction. So it was not hard to believe that the mom would not be focused on the girl, who was behaving herself. I glanced over at the girl from the bench. She was almost out of view behind a colorful display of quartz crystals.

That should have been it. Nothing more than another curiosity in a world full of them. I was about to move on and go find something to eat when I saw the man standing under a sign labeled FELDSPAR. He looked respectable—nice clothes, clean cut, baby face. In another moment, he might have been checking out the rocks or his cellphone, but at this moment, he stared directly at the little girl on her tippy toes. The expression on his face was beyond doubt. Lust. It made me queasy.

I hoped that I mistook his intentions. I went and stood directly behind him, followed his line of sight, hoping that maybe he was looking at the mother or an asteroid fragment that was mounted on the wall. But the little girl was the only object of interest visible from this angle. I did the same thing from her orientation, kneeling next to her, my dread growing at the knowledge that if she turned her head he would catch her eye. The man was wearing a blue blazer. I rummaged through his pockets. Hard candies and rabbit's feet, each in a variety of bright inviting colors. Everything about him seemed creepy and odd.

But I was hungry. And the world was frozen. It wasn't like he could snatch the girl. I reassured myself that when the world unfroze—and I still could not imagine a world in which innocence such as hers would face the unflinching reality of never growing up—she would merely walk back to her mother and the man would decide that she was not the easy target he suspected. That's what I told myself as I walked away from her.

Discussion: Your Digestive Tract and You

RESIDING IN A FROZEN world does not exempt you from basic bodily functions. You still need to take in a certain number of calories in order to sustain a basic level of daily activity. Your diet will need to remain balanced in order to be healthy.

Probably the first thing that will happen will be that you will get thirsty. Depending on where you are and your state of mind—which is likely to be somewhere between poor and apoplectic—you will rush to the nearest faucet or tap and try to turn it on. You will no doubt be shocked to find that the water inside refuses to flow. This will be the case for all sinks, showers, water fountains and sprinkler systems. This realization will lead to panic, which will make your throat go dry, which will make you considerably thirstier. All of this will make it very difficult to think straight. A person can go no more than a couple of days without fresh water before shriveling up and dying a horrible death.

When faced with a situation like this, you are going to do some things that are ridiculously off base. Don't beat yourself up about it. It doesn't really matter as long as you eventually stop acting like a moron. Preferably sometime before you shrivel up and die a horrible death. Besides, in your frozen world, there is no one else to see you being stupid, so you should be able to not care. Unless you have serious self-esteem issues, in which case living in the frozen world is going to be really hard for you. Good luck.

On the drinking issue, you may for example decide that you need to carry a bucket around and gather water from any possible source in order to ensure that you stay hydrated. It is possible that you realized early on that if you touch water you could make it flow over your fingers, into a glass and down your throat. So for a frantic few hours, you might seek out water that is already in mid-flow—drinking fountains that are in use, sinks that are open on the cold side, even water being squirted from bottles toward the mouths of those ubiquitous bike messengers. Very carefully, you can place a bucket underneath the static flow, then wave your hand through the stream, causing the water to drop with a splash into the waiting receptacle. After hours of this sort of effort, you will probably manage to fill the bucket about two inches deep.

You will be despondent. You will be certain that you are going to die.

Until you go into a 7-Eleven in search of a Big Gulp cup to have your last drink. Inside the convenience store (or supermarket or deli or anyplace that has a refrigerated case), you will remember the miracle of bottled water. Our world is literally awash in the stuff. Everyone sells it. In your previous non-frozen world, you and your friends probably mocked the insanity of people who plunked down two dollars for a few ounces of something that should be free. In the frozen world, bottled water is your lifeblood. Anywhere you go, fresh drinking water is never more than half a block away—assuming you are in a vaguely urban environment and not in the middle of somewhere like the Amazon rainforest. And it is free. Problem solved.

But you still gotta eat. You have no idea how crops get farmed and perishables packaged and meat butchered and preservatives added. So you will starve. Goodbye, cruel frozen world.

Yeah, not so much. Turns out food is hardly a challenge. At first, realizing that you cannot turn on a flame or fire up a microwave, you will panic (again!), convinced that you will never have a decent meal. But this world is not a harsh one. Lonely yes, quiet certainly, boring without doubt—but not harsh. This is not a Darwinian environment. Nothing is trying to eat you. And with no moving parts, the only true threat to you is your own stupidity.

Try this: go into a supermarket.

In a different type of apocalypse—say a world overrun with zombies or where the magnetic field has reversed polarity— after a defined period of time, vegetables and fruits and meats and dairy products and pretty much all food will go bad. It becomes inedible, which would leave only canned goods and dried sundries and other non-perishables. You might gather aluminum cans filled with fruits and vegetables and meats in a desperate effort to stockpile. It is possible you might even try cheese in a spray bottle. It will not be as good as it sounds.

Now, put your brain to work. Go back to the produce section, which is awash in glorious greens and yellows and reds with splashes of orange and purple and blue that signify the full range of nutrients you will need. Look around. You will see a stock boy unloading a crate of apples onto a shelf. One has fallen behind him. Forgive the author—that was old thinking. *Was* falling. The apple hangs there, halfway to the floor. That apple—the temptation—is your gateway to knowledge. Pluck it out of the air and take a bite. Of course it is wonderful, unblemished. Its juice will linger on your tongue, its stickiness on your lips. Taste it, smell it, feel it.

Understand this. In a frozen world, what was fresh will stay forever fresh until you eat it. What was rotten will stay rotten.

Don't eat anything out of the meat and seafood coolers. What was uncooked will remain uncooked.

This is only one supermarket in a world full of supermarkets. You will not starve.

DON'T FORGET RESTAURANTS ARE another great source of food. In the frozen world, the author has stood in countless kitchens, mesmerized by the chefs and prep cooks and waiters and busboys in their balletic tableau. How often has he coveted something that is in the process of being made, a dish that has not yet landed on a plate? But those entrees and appetizers are off limits, for there is no way to know if they are yet fit for human consumption. Stick to the food that is already on the tables. Or if knowing someone else already took a couple bites of your meal weirds you out, then look for the dishes that are just coming out of the kitchen, carried by waiters but not yet claimed by diners. You can eat at all the best restaurants in town—assuming that your world freezes at roughly lunchtime like mine did. I am still amazed when I stumble upon a new restaurant and grab a new dish and find it as ready to eat as the day it was made, which as far as I am concerned was a long time ago.

Since this is a comprehensive guide to your survival in the frozen world, the author feels compelled to raise a subject that is not often discussed in polite company. If you're gonna eat, you're gonna crap. In the interests of maintaining basic decorum, this guide will henceforth refer to the act of taking a shit with the term favored by the author's mother, "doing one's business." But you know what I mean.

I have sh— … done my business in nearly every toilet I have found. While the plumbing no longer functions, your bowels most certainly do. Food that goes in must come out. It is possible, though ill-advised, to use a toilet more than once. True, when the world springs to life anew, thousands of people will find business of unknown origin in their toilets.

But a single flush, hardly an imposition for those thousands of hands, and the business will disappear. Sure, you could do your business outside. But then you might feel compelled to walk around with little plastic bags like you're walking a dog and what are you going to do with those anyway? Put them in garbage cans? That's not much better. Besides, doing your business outside, of all the things that you could do in this situation, feels most like the end of human civilization. We are, quite simply, meant to do our business on the toilet.

It is possible to rid a toilet of your business manually. This is not possible in most public places where the toilets have all been rigged with automatic sensors and electronic flushing mechanisms. None of that works in a frozen world. Those toilets won't flush.

However, toilets of the household variety rather than commercial can function normally when forced. This is only the case for toilets that have a holding tank that fills with water instead of a pipe spewing water directly into the bowl. This construction will allow you to open the back and manually force the toilets to flush, removing all remnants of your business. It is not an easy maneuver, and is only recommended if you have found somewhere to hunker down and you wish to exist without seeing old business every time you go into the bathroom.

Here's what you do. Take the lid off the tank. If this is the first time, bail out all the standing water. Then, balancing on one foot with your knee pushing down the handle to keep the rubber stopper open, pour water directly into the pipe that leads from the tank to the bowl. Maintain a steady stream. The momentum imposed will be just enough to send the water in the bowl and the rest of the contents down into the lower pipes, headed toward, but probably never reaching the sewer. In all likelihood you will provide only enough thrust to drive your business a few feet into the pipes, where it will collect into a massive clog that will back up as soon as the other far more powerful forces of this world are unchained again. But for a brief time, you will be able to use a toilet repeatedly. As stated earlier, this is not recommended.

Pissing is another thing altogether. Do it wherever the mood strikes. Against walls. Off tall buildings. Into bushes. Onto fire hydrants. Mark the world with your scent. Have fun with it. Trust me; no one will ever know.

Notes about the Author's Father

MY FATHER IS INCAPABLE of understanding the progression of time. To him, the day is a shattered plate on the ground, never to be a cohesive whole again. He will pick up this piece or that and choose his time on that basis.

There were days in January where he would be dressed in shorts and a T-shirt, convinced it was the height of summer. Tuesday became Friday, and Friday Sunday, and so on. He would sometimes go to bed at two in the afternoon, thinking it was eleven at night.

The condition was at its worst at home when he was alone with me and my mother. That was where he would get confused. He used to be a philosophy professor at GW. The university provided him with graduate students who kept him on schedule during the work day. If you put him in a classroom and said, "Now is the time to deliver your lecture," he would know exactly where in the syllabus to pick up the thread and be able to provide an engaging dialog for a roomful of students eager to soak up his peculiar world view, delivered in his distinctive manner and wit, and answer questions without missing a beat. At these times he did not seem the least bit batshit crazy. The same if he was told, "Now you have office hours," or "Sit down at the computer and write your book," or "This is a faculty meeting." But at home he could not handle the lack of structure in his interactions with his family. For years I wondered if I was the reason he was messed up.

The shrinks could never agree on what was wrong with him. His condition defied labeling. They thought he was "high-functioning" until he wasn't. One group said it was an odd form of mania. Another called it an unusual dissociative disorder. There was the one doctor who thought my father was schizophrenic. I guess most patients don't get so much attention, but my father had achieved a certain degree of celebrity by the time he arrived at Saint Elizabeths.

It wasn't all bad. I loved him and in his way he loved me. That's the thick skin of curdled cream on top of our spoiled milk. We both could have tried harder, I suppose. But the odds were stacked against us and it didn't help that we were playing with different decks.

He did take me to the zoo sometimes. We didn't talk. I would overhear the other kids chatting with their moms and dads, the adults maintaining a constant patter about the animals.

Look at that one, isn't he cute, hi monkey, says here they're from Africa, that's very far away, maybe you'll go there someday, but I doubt it, let's go see the sea lions, where's he hiding now, oh there he is, isn't he cute.

But five-year-old me and thirty-seven-year-old him, we just strolled from pen to pen, cage to cage, in silence, as if we were at the Louvre. And the patter was all in my head as I stood beside him. I longed to be part of the monologue in his mind, to plug my earphones directly into the back of his brain and just eavesdrop. Sometimes as we stood next to each other, I wasn't sure he remembered I was there. But before he moved to the next animal, he would always glance at me—my cue that it was time to go—and I knew that he was keeping track of me.

He never held my hand as we walked, but I pretended he did.

The animals were like him. No sense of time. Just vessels for generalized and easily manipulated instincts about when and how to do things. In their natural habitats, all those impulses made sense. In the zoo, they were extraneous, but still ever present. Some of the animals got lazy, seemingly content in their easy circumstances, but most still hid when the zookeepers approached, still wanted to migrate or hunt or mate or fight or forage or wean or burrow or any number of other actions that were all completely unnecessary in the zoo. All that was really required of them was to not die and to look pretty for the good people of D.C.

So he would watch them. Particularly in the small mammal house, if he got a good stare going with a meerkat or an elephant shrew or a pale-headed saki we could stand in front of that glass divider for an hour.

I once asked my mother how they had managed to get married, have sex, raise me, and so forth. She just looked away and said, "He could be so charming."

During the span of their courtship and marriage, my father gave my mother a single present. A necklace. Actually, it's a ring. Three interlocking bands of gold, not connected to each other, but inseparable, like magician's hoops. On a finger, they nest together perfectly, creating rolling hills that can be driven up and down your skin like treads.

He told my mother that this ring could help her understand the way his mind worked. Inside him, there were different tracks, separate competing realities, each one equally real, all entwined together, connected by a coherence that only he could navigate. But the ring made too much sense on a finger, an object in context. That didn't quite fit with his metaphor—he absolutely loved metaphors. So my father bought a chain—also gold, also shiny—and he strung the ring through it. It was now a necklace, the ring hanging there weightless, untethered, a perfect representation of his state of mind.

My mother knew she shouldn't take it. She knew that this

was a moment to run from, not to embrace. But he could be charming, as she said, particularly in those early days before he truly succumbed to his illness. And that was the most vulnerable he would ever be for her.

She wore that necklace always. One night, long after the tumor had taken hold, she panicked, screaming that the necklace was gone. I assured her it was around her neck like always, picked up her hand and placed it on the ring. She rolled it between her fingers and relaxed.

"I knew I was making the biggest mistake of my life," she said, her raspy voice hinting at her joy. "And there was nothing I could do to stop it."

Nothing I could do.

On the day he gave it to her, she lowered her head and lifted the hair off the back of her neck, allowing my father to reach his hands around. His surprisingly nimble fingers latched the necklace there, letting it fall so that the ring tapped her sternum before coming to rest.

Things You Might Try to Unfreeze the World

A T SOME POINT, YOU will decide that you must do everything you can to bring the world back to life. Something that will flip the switch and power everything back up. After all, unless you have company in your frozen world—that would be awesome for you, unless of course it is someone you don't like, which would suck—you are the only one left here. Don't worry about seeming self-centered when you make it all about you. It is.

So you will start thinking of different things you could do to fire up this jalopy. In case you are having trouble brainstorming, here are some ideas to get you started.

1. Do Something Illegal (But Not Horrific).

Seriously, don't do anything you'll truly regret. Go for a misdemeanor.

For example, if you see a cop in the vicinity, walk over to said cop, take his gun out of the holster and tap him on the forehead. Remember, the goal is to get arrested, because you can only get arrested if the world unfreezes.

I may need to write a companion guide next that instructs

you what to do in the recently unfrozen world. In this case, if the cop wakes up, drop the gun and run.

(Suggestions contained in this guide should not be construed as legal opinions or taken as intelligent advice. Some of the misdemeanors cited may in fact be felonies, but without Google, well, let's just say don't count on anything being fact-checked.)

2. Do Something Embarrassing.

Put yourself in compromising positions. Do something that'll make them stand up and take notice.

The author recommends public nudity, which could also qualify for the first category.

Start out simply, say, by pulling down your pants. On the steps of the Smithsonian Air and Space Museum. In front of a tour bus full of nuns.

When they don't react, go full monty. Take it all off. Live a little. Though the author has two simple suggestions: wear shoes and sunscreen.

Note that if you happen to exist in a frozen world that is actually below freezing, nudity is not advisable. Neither is going into a prestigious law firm and dancing on their conference room table singing "Louie Louie" during a staff meeting, but you know what? Sometimes things just happen.

3. Say the Magic Word.

Sounds obvious, right? Isn't there always a word that solves the problem? Say the right word and the spell is broken. The cave with the treasure opens. The frog becomes the prince. The boy turns into the superhero. The servant girl into the belle of the ball. One word to unlock the very essence of an evil man and his troubled childhood. One word to restart the world.

Try the obvious ones: Abracadabra. Shazam. Bippity-boppity-boo. Open sesame. Rosebud. Please. I love you.

Of course, none of those will work. This may lead you to

decide to take a more methodical approach. Go to a local library. Find a dictionary—a good one, an OED, unabridged—and then take as much time as necessary to read every single word in it aloud.

The dictionary is easy to work through. Simple, logical, some big words. Find a table and drop the two tomes of the OED down with a thud. It is cathartic to make noise in a library. Though like everything else the novelty of that passes quickly.

Start to read. There are a lot of words that start with A. More than you would think. Clear your throat and intone each word deeply, like a magician who understands the trick is mostly accomplished through the presentation. Feel free to be majestic and portentous. Pause after each word and glance around at the other people in the library, providing time for them to blink and stretch and wonder why the hell they felt so stiff.

Important tip: don't read only the boldfaced words. Those are a subset of what you need to read. There are plurals and adverbs and gerunds and any other number of torturous variations of the English language. The entry for admire also includes admires, admired, admiring and so on. -ly, -ness, -ful, -less, -ish, -er, -tion … nothing can be skipped.

If you manage to read every word in the English language, there is a small possibility that one of them will be the one that restarts the world. This is only conjecture since the author only got halfway through the Fs, which was also around the time that he realized the magic world could be in French or Spanish or Swahili or Pig Latin. The original theory isn't necessarily bad, but unfortunately you are hopelessly outmatched.

4. Die.

Yeah, you'll get to this eventually. The first problem is that it is generally unsatisfying to know that if you die you won't know if it works. You'll be dead. Plus, you're probably going to have to kill yourself. Grace's brother killed himself. That was before I knew her. But he managed to do it. And the world wasn't even frozen—as far as the author knows. Bottom line is that this may be the answer, but it isn't as easy as tapping the officer with his gun.

Mise-en-scène of the Crime

I HAD DECIDED I needed to die. The logic went something like this. At the moment the world came to a halt, I was about to be killed. Maybe my survival—my refusal to die—was the pebble in the gears. It was the sheer will of my soul and body to survive that kept the machine from functioning. The mind is a powerful thing, so they tell us.

Our reality is dependent on our senses. Our senses are dependent on our brains. And if people like my father are to be believed, the brain is dependent on the spirit. In some of his later work, before the incident landed him in Saint Elizabeths, my father started to write about the power of the "spirit." That was his word for the soul. My father claimed the spirit could affect the physical world around it by the strength of its subconscious desires. Toward the end of his academic career, the journals he published in were less prestigious, the institutions publishing them sketchier. Even the paper on which his words were being printed was pulpier, scratchier. Still, my mother collected every publication he ever appeared in, reserving a shelf in the study for them. She tracked him best as an archivist, studying him with an impassive eye.

Maybe I was the manifestation of all my father's theories. After all, we share a genetic makeup. It's possible that I am merely an evolutionary step toward the proof of his theorems. I would test his assertions in a way he never could.

So I found myself back at the intersection of Wisconsin and Jenifer again. In front of that Mercedes, staring at the driver. His expression hadn't changed. The same three people stood on the curb. Their expressions were also unchanged, but now I saw a new element in each. Pity. They knew what I was trying to do. They were all waiting for me to die.

I stood there. Spoke out loud.

"I am ready to die."

Nothing happened, of course.

"Kill me. Run me over. Come on. Now is your time. Your moment. Kill me. Do it."

The driver stared at me. Stared through me.

"I will die."

I stepped forward and kicked the Mercedes' bumper, hoping the jolt would get it running again. Hurt my damn toe; no other effects.

I lay down in front of the car. Rolled myself under the front wheel. The rubber of the tire gave ever so slightly when I pressed my body against it. But it would not move. Nor would I. I was tired, and with my head under the car, there was at least some darkness to fool my body into thinking that the sun was setting. So I fell asleep there on the blacktop.

By the time I returned to the intersection, time had passed even though no time had passed at all. I had gone to sleep and woken up countless times. For a while I kept a tally, but then I lost the piece of paper with the marks and didn't try to recreate it. I was a true nomad. Like Mr. Hurwitz used to say when he found us wandering aimlessly during the school day, "What are you Bedouins up to?"

I rarely slept in the same place twice. I napped on deli counters and under park benches, at the feet of sales clerks and in the bunk beds of children, on concrete and grass and linoleum and granite and mulch and woodchips and metal and money. One of the first conventions of society that fled from me was the need to sleep in a bed. I shed it with vigor. I slept when I was tired, I woke when I was done sleeping, and at that moment under the Mercedes I was exhausted.

I woke there, staring up at the undercarriage, only somewhat aware that there were tiny pebbles embedded in my cheek, having just dreamed of being run over by a car.

I emerged at 1:17 on a sunny Thursday. Drowsy, I considered the people on the curb—the man about to dart into the street, the woman on the verge of tears, the messenger who didn't care—and couldn't remember what they had been looking at. What was I looking at? *I've finally forgotten everything*, I thought. My memory had been blissfully erased. No such luck. Sleep slipped away and returned me to my never-ending dream. About to leave, I peered again through the windshield at the man who was supposed to kill me but stubbornly refused.

The passenger side door was unlocked. I climbed in and sat next to the driver. He had a double chin straining against the top button of his shirt. Maybe he was having trouble breathing or in the midst of a heart attack. That could explain the lapse in concentration that would lead to the accident. On the floor of the car at my feet lay brochures for health clubs.

I was about to slide over a bit to get a better view out the front window from the driver's perspective, a stronger sense of whether the wheel was being turned, but something constrained me. I had put on my seatbelt. When did that happen? A completely unconscious act on my part, so strongly conditioned as to be automatic. I was about to click the button, let the strap slide across my body back into the door frame, when I was overcome by a moment of dread. My fingers hovered over the button as I ran through the scenario. I take my seatbelt off. The ordeal ends. The Mercedes plows through the intersection into … what? That bus, clearly. The passenger, who isn't wearing a seatbelt, is thrown through the window, dying instantly when his head impacts with the pavement.

Panicked, I felt my survival instinct kick in. I undid the belt quickly and threw myself from the car, rolling across the pavement like a stuntman. Then I just felt stupid.

The messenger's expression continued to annoy me. Now I thought he was laughing at my efforts. I poured a tub of salsa from the taco truck into his bag.

So that was that. I didn't want to die.

I was running out of ideas. I considered my list of theories. There were no aliens in sight. I didn't have any clue how to uncover the government conspiracy. So I chose God.

I would force God to take notice of me. Of all of us. Compel Him to acknowledge our plight.

Okay, okay, I see the inherent contradiction here. I have referred to myself as a god, the deity who has wrought this Hell on Earth. At the same time, I am about to rail against God as an external manifestation. Can God be within us and outside of us? Is it possible to know a supreme power in any way that is separate from our internal self?

My parents didn't believe in God. They thought the only purpose organized religion had ever served was to start wars. But they were viewing God as a creation that affected Men. Not as the very stuff of the universe, irrespective of our accidental consciousness.

I decided to curse God out. Force Him to acknowledge me and what He had done. My blasphemy would be so great that He would have no choice but to reveal himself to me. I was Abraham. I was Jonah. I was Job. I had been tested enough, and now it was time for God to let me off the hook.

I tried to think of an appropriate place to rail at the Supreme Being. I could go to the top of the Capitol building or the Washington Monument—as long as I didn't need to use the elevator. I could stand on the steps of the Supreme Court or prostrate myself at the feet of Abraham Lincoln. I had any number of war memorials to choose from. Would it be more powerful to face the black void of Vietnam or the open air adulation of World War II? None of it seemed right. Did I need to go to the National Cathedral? Or was that too Christian? A synagogue? A mosque? A Buddhist temple? The Scientology Center in Dupont Circle? I knew I was about to chew out God, but I didn't know where I'd find Him. Or Her. Damnit, now I was just getting off track.

So I chose a place that would have appealed to my mother. The statue of Albert Einstein. I would look for God at the feet of the man who explained the universe to us. "Dear God," I could hear my mother saying, "save us from the symbolism." With a smile, she might add, "And shield us from the irony."

I would stand before the man who explained that everything was relative. Yeah, that was a joke.

Cursing Out God: A Monologue

"GODDAMN MOTHERFUCKING SON OF a fucking son of a bitch you asshole come out and tell me what the fuck this is all about you motherfucking piece of shit sitting up there in your goddamn celestial palace clipping your fucking toenails or doing your fucking dishes or whatever the fuck it is you do up there motherfucker while we're down here just waiting for you to make up your goddamn fucking sonovabitch mind about our fate. Show yourself, dickhead! Show yourself to me, you self-righteous piece of shit! Show yourself and tell me what to do, asshole."

Nothing happens. Take a deep breath.

"Fine, you pussy, you wuss of a fucking excuse for a God, I don't give a shit if you say a goddamn word to me, you can just be alone forever. 'Cause there ain't no one down here who's gonna talk to you anymore. I was your last fucking hope 'cause without my punk ass you got no one. And guess what, motherfucker? I don't motherfucking believe in you anymore. If you don't want to fucking talk to me, then I'm not talking to you. Not a single ass-kissing word. Got that? Is that what you want? Not a fucking word. Not a fucking word."

Fall to your knees.

"Please. Help me. Please. Talk to me. Please."

Silence. The echoing drone of nothingness presses against your ears. Einstein stares over you, into the distance, the planets revolving around him. He doesn't care about you. You are now officially out of ideas.

"Fine."

Just in case:

"Sorry for the cursing."

Time to go see your father.

Why They Call Me Duck

Mrs. Haldeman, the school secretary at the D.C. public school I attended before transferring to LSGC(AWGWU), appeared in the doorway of my classroom. I had never seen her leave the front office, and would have been hard pressed to tell you whether or not she had legs. My second grade teacher, Ms. LaFontaine, spoke to her in whispered tones that were nonetheless heard clearly by everyone.

"What is he doing here?"

"He says he has a dentist appointment."

"I don't have a note."

"He didn't send a note."

"He should send a note. Did you tell him?"

"He's in the office."

Ms. LaFontaine pointed at me. She never told us what to do. She just pointed and somehow we knew what she meant. I went to get my backpack and followed Mrs. Haldeman.

My father seemed totally normal, utterly in control of his faculties. That was the first sign that something was wrong. Even at his most lucid, he was never normal.

"This is very unusual," Mrs. Haldeman said. "Parents need

to let us know in writing if a child needs to be retrieved during the school day."

She said the words "in writing" as if she was trying to scrape a film off her tongue.

"A note?" my father said.

He's going to blow it, I thought. I didn't know what he wanted, but I was invested in my father pulling it off successfully.

"A note."

"Of course," my father said, the perfect doppelganger of a repentant parent. "I understand. His mother meant to write a note, but you know how hectic life can get. Please accept my deepest apologies. We are dreadfully sorry."

Perhaps it was the word "dreadfully" that got her. It left her nowhere else to go with her scolding.

Don't ask him what time it is, I thought, unable to help glancing at the clock myself.

"Don't let it happen again," Mrs. Haldeman said.

"Never."

We stood there silently for a moment. I was sure she wouldn't let him take me. There must be a comment in my file that said my father was not mentally fit, despite being high functioning and somewhat of a genius. Surely my mother had told them never to let him take me out of school.

But all I wanted right then was to go with him wherever he wanted to go.

Mrs. Haldeman did not stop us from leaving. Outside, I squinted against the sunlight. We were free. My father's demeanor shifted. His resolute posture eroded. Even his cheeks and mouth drooped like wax under a flame. The effort had drained him; it was hard pretending to be normal.

"There's something we need to do."

I managed a word. "What?"

"Ducks."

So we were going to the zoo.

"We've come to the end," he said.

He let me sit in the front seat and didn't even tell me to put on my seatbelt. I wasn't about to argue. Usually my feet dangled in the car, but there was a shoebox there. I rested my feet on it and decided he had put it there for just that purpose. We were in uncharted territory. We had something we needed to do, and we were going to do it together. The weight of our task rested on my slight shoulders. I wondered what time of day, what season of the year he believed it to be. I understood that when we got to the end of this mission, it was not likely to be any more real than what he saw in his head. This was my chance to share some of his reality. I did not want to miss the opportunity.

Everything looked different in the front seat, closer, more dangerous, like the cockpit of an airplane. Small for my age, I could barely see out the windows. The tops of buildings, trees with no trunks, bright-blue bursts of cloudless sky. After a few minutes, stopped at a red light, I found my voice.

"Dad? Where are we going?"

"The dentist. No, no. That's not right. The lie wasn't for you. It was for them. We're going to Georgetown. To the river. To the docks."

To Georgetown. To the river. To the docks? Three places I could not remember my father ever wanting to go.

"You mean 'ducks'?"

"Yes, right, ducks."

His fingers were in constant motion, each one tapping his thumb in rapid progression, pointer, middle, ring, pinky, ring, middle, pointer and again. My father had many, many tics; this was one I hadn't seen before. His manic energy fueled mine. My leg jiggled and jostled the shoebox. Not hard enough to knock it over, just enough to tell that there was something heavy inside.

"The time has come. Time is over."

His fingers increased their pace, now both hands. My father steered the car with his palms. The car eased to a stop. I got up on my knees and finally had a proper view out the window. He had pulled up to the curb in a no parking zone. My father came around to my side of the car and opened the door. Before I got out, I noticed that he had left the keys in the ignition. He reached down and picked up the shoebox. With his other hand, he took my arm and led me toward the river. His fingers continued their interminable march, though now they tapped the thin exposed skin of my wrist rather than his thumb. It tickled a little, but I didn't want to laugh for fear that I would break the spell.

"We need an ark. For the flood."

He wasn't looking at me and I wasn't sure who he was talking to. My father stared straight ahead as we walked, looking so far out into the distance that I thought he might trip over the curb. But he jumped it with a little spring in his step and continued toward the water.

The word "ark" didn't mean a lot to me. In our house, we had twenty-two versions of the Bible—different translations, interpretations, fonts. My parents did not believe in God, but they felt it was important to understand the context of the beliefs of others.

I would later learn that when my mother found out my father had taken me out of school, she had raced home, hoping to find us there. My father had neatly arranged the Bibles on the floor of the living room, like tiles, each one open to the story of Noah. As far as I knew, Noah was just the kid who sat at my table and clicked his tongue whenever he did math problems.

Still, we were at the water and he mentioned a flood, so I was smart enough to figure out he was talking about a boat. Down river, there was a latticework of piers for motorboats. Many of the spaces were vacant, the usual occupants dotting the river.

My father led me to a place where a concrete driveway descended into the water. A boat headed right for us. It wasn't slowing down, ready to beach itself. I tried to back away, but my father held me there.

That was when I noticed that he had dropped the shoebox and was holding a gun. I had never seen a real gun. My parents, in addition to being atheists, were pacifists. Seeing the weapon in my father's hand startled me even more than the angry boat barreling down on us.

The amphibious creature burst out of the river in a plume of spray, soaking us. A horn blasted in our faces as the boat came to an abrupt halt half in, half out of the water. I found myself facing massive truck tires. A dozen tourists poked their heads out from under the canopied midsection. A young guy, flustered, appeared above us.

"What the hell are you doing there? I coulda run you down. Lucky I saw you!"

My father said nothing, waiting.

The Ducks are one of those tourist things that we locals make fun of. Taking a tour of the city in a boat that can also drive on land. But I guess it is pretty cool to see D.C. from the Potomac and Pennsylvania Avenue.

"Get outta the way!"

The kid's voice cracked when he tried to be authoritative. There was a murmur on the boat. Pictures were taken of me and my father, the big incident on their tour of Washington D.C.

"He's got a gun," one of the tourists screamed.

The guy was right, of course, but I hadn't really thought of it that way.

My father had a gun.

I looked up into my father's face and I remember distinctly that he was smiling. It was not an expression I saw often those days. He let go of my arm and climbed up a ladder onto the deck of the boat. Like a superhero. Like a pirate.

He pulled me up next to him on the deck with surprising strength. At least that's what I remember—being lifted off my feet, taking flight momentarily then touching down by my father's side. Thinking about it later, I realized I probably went up the ladder too.

"I don't have the money on the boat, man," the tour guide said.

"We don't want money," my father said. "We need the vehicle."

It was like being in an action movie. We needed the vehicle. My dad was the hero. I was the sidekick.

The tourists retreated to the rear and started scrambling down another ladder, splashing in the water as they landed. They didn't start taking pictures again until they were clear of the boat, mistakenly believing they were beyond the gun's range. My father motioned for the tour guide to abandon ship.

"Man, you're gonna get me fired."

My father glanced at me and winked. He was playing a role, just like he had at my school, layering a patina of someone else over his churning self.

"Would it help if I shot you?" he said with a smile.

The tour guide vaulted over the side. My dad took to the wheel and the boat jerked fully onto dry land, completing its transformation. We barreled into the street, bringing cars to a screeching halt.

On land the Duck was the size of a small bus. My father's fingers tapped the steering wheel as he focused on the road. He never slowed down. Traffic laws became meaningless. The boat shuddered as my father maneuvered it around all obstacles. When he laid on the horn, our chariot bellowed with rage and indignation—a beautiful, terrifying sound. The tires bounced along the pavement, gentle undulating waves that made me feel like either we were still on the water or about to take flight. The gun clattered around uselessly at our feet.

The cops caught up with us as we swerved onto Pennsylvania Avenue. Two cars blocked the road; they didn't want us to get to the White House. Looking at the determination on my father's face, I thought he might barrel through the police cruisers, but he took a sharp turn down 19th instead. People stopped and stared at the odd retinue—our amphibious vehicle trailed by a police escort. I waved like a celebrity marshal at the Cherry Blossom Parade.

On Constitution Avenue, more cops were waiting—another roadblock, more formidable this time. The boat groaned when my dad forced it to jump the curb near the American History Museum. The grass of the National Mall was less taxing on its axles. I heard sirens all around, but the cops were not willing to follow us down the center of the Mall. I stuck my head out beyond the windshield, letting the wind hit me full force in the face. I soaked in the confused expressions of the tourists and congressional aides as we soared toward the Capitol building, the hulking edifices of the Smithsonian museums all around us.

As we crossed one more street nearing the Capitol, shots were fired. I hit the deck and clung to a life preserver. Turns out they were shooting at our tires and managed to hit one.

The Duck crashed to a halt in the middle of the Capitol reflecting pool. It was not deep enough to float in, but I felt like we were rocking on the open sea nonetheless. The standoff lasted for three hours. The police said they didn't know where the gun was and didn't want to risk my life. I found that funny; I was never in any danger. Finally, they handed my mother a megaphone and let her talk my father out of his ark. But for those three hours, he and I sat on an uncomfortable bench under that canopy, in plain sight of the TV cameras, waiting for the flood that never came.

It was on all the channels for a couple of days, those pictures of me and my father driving through the streets of downtown D.C. in our boat-car. My mother did not believe in hiding things from children, so we watched the coverage together. I didn't realize how dangerous our journey had been until I saw the footage. In particular, they kept showing one clip where we almost ran down a family of four, including a little girl my age and a baby in a stroller.

"That's why he's in jail," my mother would say after we watched another report.

The trial and sentencing came about six months later. It was relatively quick. My mother sat in the front row for the whole proceeding, but left me in school to suffer the torment of my peers. I had been branded. Before it happened, I was anonymous, just one of the guys in the class, but afterward I stood out. The boy with the crazy dad.

I'm not sure I would have survived if my mom had left me in my first school. She spent every bit of her capital with the GW Administration to get me into LSGC(AWGWU). Of course, that wouldn't have gone any better if it hadn't been for Carlos, but now I'm just repeating stories I've already told.

Discussion: Time

THE NEED TO MARK time is imprinted on the souls of men. I think that someone once said that, but if not, someone should have. Hell, I just did.

For a while, I collected watches, looking for one old-fashioned enough to wind. Something I could force my will upon. Spin the mechanism and let the gears do the rest. I never found one. The difference between noon and midnight is not so much determined by our clocks as by our definitions of noon and midnight. Noon is the time to sit and eat lunch. Midnight is the time to sleep or watch late-night TV. Noon is a time to engage with those around us; midnight is a time to wonder why we bother. Ultimately, I decided that if I found an appropriate watch, I would restart time right where it stopped—1:17 p.m.— and let my life proceed from that moment, hewing closely to the conventions of whatever hour my watch declared it to be. I would wake at 7 a.m., eat breakfast at 8 a.m., lunch at noon, dinner at 7 p.m., and go to bed by 11 p.m., then repeat the next day. I made this decision consciously, declared it out loud to the room full of statues in the food court where I happened to be sitting, then promptly gave up my search for a watch.

I holed up in a toy store for a while, taking each child's game off the shelf and learning to play them in turn. I went in order of age appropriateness: three and up, five and up, eight and up, eleven and up. I unwrapped the next game immediately upon finishing with the last. I carefully read the directions and diligently played them all. Seriously, every one on the shelf. I slept there on the floor of the toy store. And when I woke I continued through the stacks of cardboard boxes. When I completed a game, I would put it away, just as I was taught as a child, every single piece, before adding the box to the tower of games I was building off to the side. By the end, there were three towers, each precariously balanced, liable to fall at any moment. I built each one up to the height of my outstretched hand. I counted them, of course: 167 games in all.

My genes predispose me to be both obsessive and manic.

Actually, I didn't put all the pieces away. Whenever I encountered an hourglass, I would leave it out. In the end, I had a motley collection of forty-six miniature timekeepers lined up like disheveled toy soldiers—poorly trained, unable to hold the line. Each one of these hourglasses would, if flipped over, mark a specific amount of time. At first, they did not want to perform for me, but a good shake changed their minds. I had no idea how long each ran for, and for a long time—or maybe a short time, who knows?—I just lay on the floor, turning them over, one after another, watching the grains of sand or silica or whatever, drift downward as time passed. But ultimately it was chaos, each soldier marching to its own beat, ending its exercises at a different interval. It became a game, never letting one be inactive for more than a moment. Never letting time stop.

But this is a world without distractions and that makes it hard to maintain concentration. I found that more and more of the hourglasses would remain unturned for longer, until eventually all of them were spent. This particular game had ceased to be fun.

I had an idea. I would connect all the hourglasses together in an elaborate Rube Goldberg device, so that, like dominos, when one reached the end of its timekeeping, it would automatically flip the next. If I counted out the seconds each lasted, then added them all together—a simple process—I would know exactly how long my improvised clock would reckon before it needed to be reset.

But then I went to sleep again and when I woke up I was hungry. There was no food in the toy store besides the packets of gummy worms I had already eaten, so I left. As far as I know the army of impotent timekeepers still stand watch there.

If you count to sixty, you have passed one minute. If you count to three thousand six hundred, an hour. Count to eighty-six thousand four hundred and you've got yourself a day. I resolved to do that once, but the mind wanders. I did count all the way through a day, but decided that it did not need to be accomplished consecutively. I would count to a certain point—say, fourteen thousand two hundred and fifteen—write that number down and go do something else. In this way, I fractured my single day, but completed it nonetheless.

Mise-en-scène: St. Elizabeths Government Hospital for the Insane

IN FOURTH GRADE I had to write a report about a Washington landmark. I chose Saint Elizabeths. Founded in 1855, it originally went by the catchy moniker of the Government Hospital for the Insane. During the Civil War, soldiers weren't thrilled to tell their loved ones they were in the loony bin, so they started calling it Saint Elizabeths. Definitely an improvement. This is where they sent John Hinckley after he shot Reagan. My report was full of glorious facts and interesting tidbits, an elementary school epic. While proofreading my work, I arrived at the last line.

My father lives there.

I didn't even remember writing it. Maybe it was true what they said about me. Maybe I was insane too. I put my five-page masterpiece in a drawer and scribbled out a page on the Lincoln Memorial instead.

It was a long ride across the city to get to the grounds of Saint Elizabeths. I was exhausted when I arrived on the far side of the Anacostia River. I stood in front of the original building at Saint Es, in all its red majesty. It looked like a castle and I imagined myself a knight, coming to save the kingdom from the wicked spell that has befallen it. They say Saint Elizabeth—the saint, not the hospital—once healed a leper by putting him in the king's bed. She ended a famine by stealing bread from the royal larder. Incongruous actions with beneficial results. That's what I needed.

But my father was not housed in the castle. That building is crumbling and condemned.

I had not been to visit my father in many years and I counted on my memory to guide me to his room, which was a short walk away in an undistinguished building. Still, luck was with me, in some form. I found the front door to my father's building being held open by a frozen young woman who was to all appearances sane. Inside, walking through the corridors, I was struck by how few barriers I encountered between me and my father's room. Seemed like there should be bars and guards and attack dogs. Nope. Just boring hallways that smelled like Lysol.

His door was closed. I touched my fingertips to it, hoping to feel vibrations. I pressed my ear against it, listening for a sound. Any sign of life. But there was no movement.

This is what I dreaded. I tried not to believe it, but part of me could not help but think that the key to ending this ordeal was locked in my father's brain. That his madness had done this to me and the world. He might not be able to articulate how to change the circumstances, but I could figure that out by working with him. We could unfreeze the planet. We could save humanity. Me and my father. Together.

My worst fear was that I was wrong. That I would find him and nothing would change. That he wouldn't move.

And he didn't.

My father sat in the middle of his room on a small chair at a small table. The rest of the furniture—a bed, an end table, a desk—had all been pushed into the corners of the room, as far away from the center as possible. My father wore boxer shorts and a bathrobe that had fallen open to reveal a bramble of gray chest hair. His feet were bare. Bald on top, the sides of his head bristled with unruly hairs that stuck out at all angles, stiff and upright. I did not smell him until I came close enough to disrupt the space around him. He reeked of disrepair and neglect. Despite all evidence to the contrary, I hoped that maybe he was just sitting very still, possibly spooked by my arrival, a nervous creature waiting to run. Or maybe he was so lost in thought that he was simulating the immobility of the surrounding world.

I snapped my fingers in front of his face. I poked him in the arm. I kicked his shin. I yelled in his ear.

He did not move.

My father's table was piled high with magazines. More rested at his feet. They were on his bed and under it. Those that were on the table were pristine, untouched, unlike the magazines scattered elsewhere. Those had already received their treatment on my father's autopsy table, each one dissected and tossed away in tatters, all the interesting and compelling words torn from their pages, leaving only empty cadavers, shells of former selves.

There were four pairs of children's scissors lined up on the table and one in my father's hand. He held a magazine and was in mid-cut, forever. The scissors were harmless, rounded to such a ridiculous degree that his own fingers had a greater chance of harming him. The rest of my father's equipment consisted of seven rolls of Scotch tape, removed from their dispensers and stacked neatly on the table like a tower of discarded tires.

The words. Yes, the words. He had taped them up everywhere he could reach, layer upon layer. All of the magazines were filled with supermodels and gossip: *Elle, InStyle, Vogue, People, Us Weekly, Lucky*. My father ignored the pictures. It was the platitudes he wanted. The headlines. The admonitions and the advice. The wisdom.

There was no rhythm or order to how the scraps of paper were pasted to the walls. Pure chaos ruled. I felt as if I was reading the dictionary again, except that the book had exploded and buried me in its rubble, splattering its guts on every available surface. This must have been going on for years.

I wanted to track down my father's psychiatrist and give him a good shake.

The wallpaper my father had created was at least four, five, six layers deep. Even the window had been covered over, filtering the bright light through the haze of my father's search for meaning. And that's clearly what it was. He was looking for some context in the pages of *Cosmopolitan*.

I scanned the walls, hoping that he had found it. The Rosetta Stone. The key.

But I couldn't discern any meaning in those first few minutes, or were they hours? I lay down on his bed, atop the various scraps that had fallen like autumn leaves, and stared up into the canopy of his mind. I expected the edges of the paper to sway softly in a gentle breeze, but like everything else they were static.

Staring at the back of my father's head, I suddenly craved light. The shreds of paper ripped off the window easily under my fingertips, leaving flecks of tape and adhesive smudges behind. It must have taken months, maybe years to so thoroughly cover that pane of glass with those words—hundreds of strips woven together into a meaningless mosaic. I stood on the bed and tore it all off, working methodically from the top to the bottom, raining confetti down on the bed below, and in a fraction of the time all my father's work was undone.

It was a beautiful day outside. Seventy-one degrees and sunny. The view from my father's room was spectacular. Saint Elizabeths sits up on a hill overlooking the city. From here, all the landmarks were visible, appearing as a scale model before me. I imagined him looking out this window at the people and the activity, feeling omnipotent and being completely unable to handle it. The world needed to be covered up, papered over. Without context, it made no sense.

I looked down at my feet. The scraps of paper tickled my toes like freshly mown grass. Some had fallen face up, readable; some face down, inscrutable. And from the jumble, words popped out at me, phrases.

Make a Fresh Start! Is She Or Isn't She? Don't Let Your Money Manage You! Time Can Be Your Ally! Are You Sure? Basic Hygiene Tips Most Of Us Forget! Drive Him Wild! Success! Be Your Best You!

Gibberish. Useless.

Frustrated, I kicked the paper off the bed and watched it flutter to the floor. All this time, everything I had done, had been for nothing. I was no closer to understanding anything and I wasn't particularly impressed by my attempts. The world needed me and I was the wrong man for the job.

There was a watch on my father's bedside table. I don't know what it was doing there. Surely my father never wore it. Maybe it was another poor attempt by his doctors at therapy. Maybe it had been a long-ago gift from my mother that had never moved from the spot where she last placed it. I looked at it. According to this watch, the time was 7:36. It was uncommunicative on the question of a.m. or p.m.

I picked up the watch and threw it at my father. It struck him in the back of the head and fell to the floor, as worthless as it had been a moment before.

"Come on, old man. Wake up and tell me what to do."

My father did not move.

I was going to leave. And I didn't know where I would go next. But first, I knelt down to pick up the watch. It had landed on a cluster of paper—how could it have done otherwise? For no good reason, I put the watch on my wrist.

Find The Answers You Seek!

Those words stared up at me. Maddeningly cryptic, but no less heartening. Maybe there were signs to follow here. Guidance to be found. Something that would rise out of the silence in this room and make itself known.

Standing next to my father, I looked over his shoulder. He was cutting, of course. The scissors with the fuchsia handle underlined the phrase perfectly, the words he was cutting out at the moment he was ensnared in this web. In all capitals, seven letters, two words. A mission, a purpose. SAVE HER. His thumb covered the rest of the headline—FROM HERSELF— so I ignored it. The article was about staging an intervention. But that was all irrelevant to me. My father had sent me a sign.

Discussion: Sleep and Dreams

SLEEP WILL BE THE most difficult adjustment for you in your frozen world. Your body clock is hardwired to react to light and dark in order to understand when to sleep. But the frozen world will naturally be either a land of the perpetual sun or the endless night. Unless you are lucky enough to have frozen at dusk or dawn. That would have been nice.

If you freeze during daylight hours, at first when you feel yourself tiring, you can attempt to go into a room in which no lights are on and close the curtains. Pretend that in fact night has fallen and therefore the natural thing to do is to go to sleep. You will wake up after an undetermined amount of time. Do not try to figure out how long it has been. You will never know how long you have been asleep. Throw open the curtains and greet the morning, which of course will be no different from the night or the day before. Try to be enthusiastic. It won't last.

If you are stubborn, you can keep a sleep journal. Base your notes on the assumption that about twelve-sixteen hours of wakefulness are followed by eight-ten hours of sleep. This will be a rough simulation of normal circadian rhythms. The author attempted this and once tallied up seventy-two "days."

You should not feel that you have to carry on the charade for that long. This is not a competition. At some point you will give up and sleep when you are tired and not give a crap about the light anymore.

There are different kinds of dreams.

First are the hopes and aspirations of waking dreams. The kind that your guidance counselor, Miss Wadsworth, referred to when she asked about your dreams. This question may have caught you by surprise since you were under the impression that this was supposed to be a meeting to talk about options for college. But that was how she wanted to start, so whatever. Unfortunately, your mind went totally blank and you couldn't even come up with some bullshit like "I want to be a doctor" or "I see myself on stage accepting the Pulitzer" or two words: "world peace." Nothing. Nothing came to mind at all. And this was before your mom got sick so you couldn't even use that excuse. This moment would be good preparation for your frozen world, because when Miss Wadsworth gave you an icy stare, time might as well have stopped in the face of her disapproval and disappointment. And you thought guidance counselors were there to lend support.

Turns out they are there to slowly lay out brochures for safety schools.

If you are lucky, your dreams while you sleep will become a refuge. In them, everything will move and you can be as still as you like.

Here is one dream that the author has frequently in his frozen world.

The author finds himself in a rowboat. Out in the middle of a vast ocean. Frozen waves, water immobile, air stagnant. There is a hole in the bottom of his dinghy. He can see the water through it. He sticks his finger in the hole, not to plug it, but to allow the water to move. Swaying back and forth, he rocks the boat to force the water around it to lap its sides. The boat capsizes and the ocean pulls him in, swirling again.

The author always wakes up before he drowns, fully aware that he didn't fall out of the boat. He jumped.

Why You Should Never Sleep in Someone Else's Bed

I STAYED AT ST. Elizabeths for a few days. Well, I don't really know if it was days. I went to sleep a few times. I woke up a few times still in the hospital. I had left my dad's room and I didn't go back. There wasn't anything else there for me to see. Maybe I was hanging out in case he started moving and came to find me. It seemed less hopeless to explore the other hospital buildings than to stay in his room and stare at him. Which is what I would have done. Just sit on the edge of his bed and stare at the back of his head, alternately spacing out and concentrating too hard on waking him up. Of course, I also knew that if only he moved and the rest of the world stayed immobile that would be weird and complicated. Would he be insufferable because this was all something he'd predicted? Or would he lose it completely and try to stab me with a spork (which seemed to be the only type of utensil I could find in the whole complex)? Most likely I would just get an incomprehensible lecture and then he'd go back to making collages out of the words in fashion magazines.

So I wandered and I waited. This turned out to be a really stupid idea.

St. Elizabeths is a hospital. A mental hospital, sure. But still a hospital. I should have thought about that when I was getting into beds to sleep without regard to who might have been in them before me. Eating the food off trays I found, not caring too much about who I was swapping spit with. You see, people live in that hospital, but they also get sick and are treated and die there. I should have realized all that.

But I didn't. Live and learn. Unless the learning kills you.

After a few times sleeping in some beds with sheets of questionable provenance (though to my credit I did avoid the ones with obvious stains or moist spots), I got bored and left St. Es.

The first thing I noticed as I got back on my bike is that the world had gotten warmer. But that wasn't possible. Still, even before I started pedaling back across the river, I was starting to sweat. I considered the possibility that in fact the world wasn't in stasis, but was just changing very slowly and that the gradations in temperature were discernible.

Then it got a lot colder. Somewhere around the Washington Monument, I began to shiver uncontrollably. I was coasting down a small hill with the White House in front of me when the world spun out and took me down.

The sound of my own breathing brought me around later. I didn't know how long I had been lying there. My breaths burst out of me, staccato, like a steam train, huff, huff, huff. Or a dying dog. Short, wet, angry. A metallic taste on my tongue. Blood. My own. I licked the corner of my mouth and found the source. My cheek was wet. My arm didn't want to move, but I forced the issue and gently ran my fingers across my face. They came back red. I could see, which was good. Though I had a little trouble focusing. My bike was on its side. The front wheel was still spinning. Couldn't have been unconscious for that long.

The side of my face stung. My whole side ached. I pushed on each tooth with my tongue to see if any were loose or missing.

All there. Not sure why that was what I thought I needed to do, but it made me feel a little better to find a full set.

How could I be sick? In a frozen world, wouldn't viruses and bacteria be frozen too? Unless the exception was whatever was symbiotic with me. If it was a virus, it must have been there, gestating, since before the world froze. Or maybe once something got inside me, my own systems betrayed me and woke it up.

I sat up. Except that I didn't. I propped myself up on my elbow, but as soon as my head came off the ground, the world pitched and swirled around me. I fell back and discovered that my shoulder and my ankle also hurt. My eyes closed in an attempt to shut out the stimuli of the rocking world, now in full unwelcome motion around me. It didn't help at all—the gyroscope in my brain continued to spin. My hand grabbed for my face. I was trying to cover my eyes, I think, but ended up slapping my nose, which resulted in yet another place I hurt. My fingertips on my forehead recoiled from the heat.

A fever. An accident. No way to know which was responsible for what. But in just a few seconds, I had gone from stable to critical condition. Bones might be broken. There might be internal bleeding. I might have a horrible virus and need intravenous fluids and an aggressive treatment of experimental antibiotics.

I needed to go to the hospital. I had completely forgotten that I was coming from a hospital. "You just need to move slower," I said to myself, opening my eyes again. It was true. When I concentrated on keeping my movements deliberate, I could control the tilt of the world. It was still swaying, but it was like the teacups at Disneyland—they always spin, but if you grab that wheel in the middle of your compartment you can make it go psycho, which some people like, but I never did. "Don't spin the teacup," I told myself.

Moving like a Zen tortoise, I managed to get to my feet. I had a new goal. GW hospital. I shuffled on autopilot back toward the campus. I had been on so many field trips and other outings in this area that I could focus mainly on not falling over rather than navigating. I felt every drop of sweat leave my body and claw its way into the fabric of my shirt. Sometimes I stumbled along with one eye closed; depth perception made everything worse. I stopped frequently to lean on delivery trucks, parking meters, historical markers.

I was convinced that everyone was watching me. They weren't frozen. They were transfixed by the spectacle of the boy straggling along like a zombie. *Drunk*, they probably thought, *or worse. Coke?* one asked the other. *LSD*, came the response. *I'm in trouble*, I wanted to yell, when no one helped me. But the effort was too great. I heard the syncopated brush of my shoes on the pavement. I felt like I was breathing out of my ears, rather than my mouth and nose, but at least I had stopped panting.

Just get to the hospital. They will help you there.

Like they helped your mom? a little voice asked. Yeah, not like that.

Shuffle, shuffle, shuffle. One foot in front of the other.

The blue sky filled with purple spots and the clouds began to drip like candles on a hot stove. More voices in my ears, all the people around me whispering. But when I fixed my gaze on any one of them, they froze again. It was only behind my back that they moved and laughed. When I did look at them, their eyes glowed red and their skin looked like granite. I expected them to crack. Not like giving in and moving and telling me it was all a big joke, but to actually break into pieces and crumble to the ground. Under their clothes, I believed that they were covered with welts and boils and bursting pustules. It made me itchy and nauseous.

Don't look at anyone. Keep walking.

I was off the Mall now, surrounded by large buildings again. The shadows reached for me. I avoided the dark patches on the ground, thinking I would fall into a deep abyss and drown.

There were millipedes jousting in my abdomen. Somewhere on 20th Street, my eyes rolled upward into a blinding light, and when I was able to see again I was staring into the depths of a GW trash can that was now covered with my vomit.

Keep walking. Shuffle on.

A quad full of students. Squinting, I heard music. R.E.M. were playing "So. Central Rain" in a free outdoor concert and all the college kids around me were swaying and smiling and I was one of them and my mom was dancing there too in a completely embarrassing mom way but I had never been happier to see her because it meant she wasn't dead but she was and when I stopped squinting R.E.M. was gone and so were all the students and I was standing in front of the doors to the GW emergency room.

The doors were open. A gurney with a man hooked to an IV and a respirator was halfway over the threshold. I shuffled past him, looking for a doctor or nurse who moved.

The last thing I remembered was throwing up into the soft soil at the base of a ficus tree.

The Hallucination That Played on Infinite Loop While I Was Feverish That Wasn't Actually a Hallucination But a Memory I Wish I Could Forget

"I HAVE TO GO."

Her voice was so weak in those last weeks that sometimes when I heard it I didn't recognize it, mistaking it for a thought of my own.

I had been reading in the corner chair of her room, dozing between paragraphs. My mother always had a stack of books on her nightstand, sometimes so many that one was hard pressed to identify the piece of furniture beneath them. When she was moved from her room upstairs into the office, into that hospital bed, I gathered the books from her to-do pile, fifteen in all, and started to read them. My original thought was to read them aloud to her, but I found myself reading silently in her presence and feeling that was enough. She would often just stare at the ceiling, eyes half closed, breathing in the rasp that had become background noise like the hum of the air conditioning units. I was working on *A History of God*, a book my mother had added back to the pile for a second reading on the night she was diagnosed with the tumor. I could barely get through three pages without falling asleep—no disrespect to the author, but it had become my most reliable sedative.

"I have to go."

A little stronger, the voice, a little more urgent.

I sat up. She was trying to raise her head. She could maintain a seated position and feed herself simple foods without sauces, change the channels on the TV if the remote was placed in her hand and her finger guided to the right buttons—though all those abilities, one by one, in inevitable succession, would soon be taken from her. But moving from a reclining position to a seated one is harder than it looks, the number of muscles involved, the order of operations that need to be sequenced properly. This was something she could not do anymore. I hurried over to her side, pulled her up toward me into an embrace and organized the pillows behind her—actions that had become reflexive to me.

"Do you want some water?"

"I … have to … go."

I had moved her too fast and she was laboring for breath. I was still dazed, not yet fully awake, and I chastised myself for not being more careful. I listened to her words for the first time.

The portable toilet was in the opposite corner of the room. At this point, I was only alone with my mother overnight. We had nurses come in during waking hours, but the dead of night was still my responsibility until help arrived the next morning. I had seen them—my mother and the nurses—struggle to use the toilet. They would lift her and I could tell that she would chafe at the indignity and I would hurry away to another part of the house, ashamed that I had seen even that much. She had never needed me to help her. She had always slept straight through the night.

Until now.

I dragged the toilet over. Nothing more than a plastic bowl in a metal frame that looked too flimsy to hold any real weight. The rubber disks on the bottoms of the legs caught on the rug, bunching it up, slowing my progress as I had to lift up the toilet and smooth out the folds. I was panicking and I knew it, which added to my frustration.

My mother was whimpering softly now. Her instincts, what was left of her pride made her struggle to hold back her bowels.

"Okay, we're gonna do this. Okay?"

She looked at me and leaned forward, falling into my arms. I steadied her with my body, her head on my shoulder, and swung her legs off the bed. Immediately, I could feel her full weight against me. Her muscles were slack. This was going to be a game of one on one, me versus gravity.

It was only four feet to the toilet. Two feet to the right and two feet down. I told her that we'd take the hypotenuse express to get us there faster. It was the type of joke that would have made her laugh just a couple of months earlier. Instead she was panting, her breath hot and wet on my neck, quivering. I saw the entire operation in my mind: lift, pivot, lower. *Piece of cake*, I told myself.

"Here we go."

I hooked my elbows under her armpits, but I'd misjudged. She was heavier than I remembered and I almost dropped her. Her legs were of no use to us. I found myself in a squat, demanding that willpower alone keep us both from falling to the floor. That was when she started to cry.

"It's okay. We're okay."

My words did not reassure her or me. I summoned some reserve of strength and forced us back into a standing position, both of us expelling sharp gasps of air. My mother stiffened, jarred by the sudden movement. Her tears, her breathing, everything stopped for a moment. I took advantage of her temporary rigor mortis to pivot toward the toilet—it was easier to move her clenched up. We were almost there. I bunched her gown up to her waist and started to lower her to the bowl. I didn't want to look at her nakedness—I had not broken through that wall yet, though that barrier would shatter soon. And so, she was almost seated when I realized she was wearing underwear.

I dropped my shoulder down to her midsection, too hard, too fast, but that was the only way to continue to support her weight and have both hands on the elastic of her underwear. I could feel the wind get knocked out of her. I was operating on instinct, trying to get this done before the shame of my actions overcame me and drove me into a state of useless embarrassment. I thrust my hands downward, pulling the underwear past her thighs and calves to her ankles.

Her entire body relaxed. It was too late. My mother did not eat much anymore and what came out was watery, running down her leg, leaving little pieces of shit on her skin as it went. I threw her down onto the bowl, where most of the mess landed. When I placed her hands on the railing, her fingers grabbed on, gripping like talons, finally exerting some strength, some control as she held herself upright.

I backed away, sat on the floor against the wall, collapsed there and stared straight into her face, framed by the stringy white hair that had once been thick and auburn, and we both ignored what was below, the puddle on the hand-woven rug, the stickiness glistening on her legs. We were catching our breath, for just a brief time unable to move as she relieved herself and I avoided all thoughts of being only halfway done. We would still need to clean ourselves up. The soiled underwear would have to be replaced and the new pair properly positioned. She would have to stand and pivot and fall into bed. All this lay before us. For hours, for days, for her last weeks, so much more of that was ahead of us.

What had happened tonight would not be repeated. Once I told the nurse, diapers and bedpans appeared. More indignities.

We were still. Each in our own way considering that this moment would now bound our relationship, that this moment would redefine far too much of our past, driving out an unacceptable number of fading memories. It was not fair, and we both knew it. There was nothing to be done except move forward. Let time's incessant march take us to the destination we both knew was coming, one step at a time.

I did not cry until she was back in bed and the bowl was emptied, until the room was cleaned and smelled of disinfectant rather than shit, until I had showered the filth off of me and gotten into my own bed, until the lights were off and I was drifting downward to sleep, until my head was on the pillow and it could sponge up my tears.

Someone Moves

THE DROPLET OF WATER drifted lazily down the side of the orange plastic cup, cutting a path through the condensation. I could see it clearly, though everything around it was blurry. I closed my eyes, squeezed them tight, trying to understand where I was. When I opened them again, nothing had changed except that the drop had moved a few more millimeters, almost reaching the table at the base of the cup, where it would merge with an existing ring of moisture.

I hurt in many places. There was a rasp to my breathing and my throat felt scraped raw. My tongue was dry. I forced myself to sit up, each movement highlighting a different aching body part. The water was cold. I drank slowly through a straw.

The rest of the room came into focus. I was a bit woozy. A hospital suite. There were two other beds lined up next to mine, both empty. The curtains between them were open. The shades were drawn across the window—that explained the darkness. The cool wet surface of the cup felt so good on my hand that I rolled it across my forehead, lingering on my temples.

TAKE THESE NOW.

The note was written on a small piece of paper on the table

next to the water ring left by the cup. All uppercase block letters.
Two pills partially covered the H and the O. I picked them up
and popped them in my mouth without thinking. They were
halfway down my throat before I wondered if that was a good
idea. I hoped they were painkillers, but somehow I knew they
were antibiotics. I picked up the note—it was written on the
back of a blank prescription form for a thoracic surgeon based
at GW hospital.

There was another note on the table on a second piece of
paper from the same pad: TAKE THESE LATER. Two more
pills. I put them in my pocket. I was wearing my clothes, no
hospital gown.

I tried to remember how I got there. Everything was a bit
fuzzy, a long waking dream that had lasted my whole life. I
tried to focus on recent events—what was real, what wasn't.
A frozen world. Perhaps. Yet the water was cold; the droplet
moved. Someone had filled the cup. Someone had written the
notes. Someone was taking care of me.

Maybe it was over.

I stood up too fast and had to grab the side of the bed to
regain my balance. My shoes were still on. There was no one
else in the room. I shuffled to the door and looked out into
the hallway. Plenty of people out there. A nurse pushing
a wheelchair-bound octogenarian. A doctor talking to a
teenager. A guy in pink scrubs wearing a clown's nose. None
of them moved.

Fuck me.

I went back into my room, feeling dejected. The dreams were
real. I tried to piece together my time in the hospital. Throwing
up. A lot. That I remembered. I went in the bathroom. It
smelled like vomit, but was clean. There was another note
taped to the mirror.

MEET ME IN 649.

Meet me. Someone else. The cold water by the bed. No
vomit on the floor. The world was frozen, but I was not alone.

Someone else had moved. Someone else had left me a note and told me where to find him. Or her.

I raced back into the hallway, looking desperately for a hospital floor plan on the wall. I needed directions. Halfway down the hall, I realized I should look at a room number: 422. Inside that room, a woman stood next to the bed of a man who had no hair. Not a balding man—a chemotherapy patient. Off to the side, another woman held a balloon and looked awkwardly at the string. The balloon was a mistake, she realized at the moment time stopped. But she was stuck with it. Forever. They all looked sad and it reminded me that my mom was dead but that wasn't what was happening right now. Right now, someone else was moving. Someone was waiting for me in 649.

I found an elevator and jammed on the up button repeatedly. The digital numbers next to the door displayed 8. I waited. It didn't change. I pushed the button so hard I hurt my thumb and only then remembered that elevators don't move.

Stairs. I burst through the door into the stairwell. Sprinted up two flights. Had a moment where I thought the door might be locked from the outside and I would be stuck inside forever, knowing I had lost my only chance at human contact. The door opened. I was on the sixth floor.

Around a corner—637, 639, 651. What?

I went back. Down a side hall—648, 642. Who the hell numbered the rooms in this place? The side hall dead-ended into room 604. Seriously?

Retracing my steps, I finally found a schematic of the floor. It showed all the fire exits and if I squinted I could read the tiny room numbers.

Room 649 was huge and right around the corner. I took a deep breath and went to meet the only other person who understood what I was going through. I hoped it was a doctor or better yet a hot nurse. Someone who could take care of me next time I got sick. But I was overwhelmed by the fear that it was going to be someone like that creepy hospital clown and that my little story was about to take a horrific turn that would have been totally hilarious in a movie but was really really not funny in real life.

I found myself in a small room outside the main room. There was a bank of sinks here. A wall of windows allowed a nurse who was frozen in mid-scrub to see into the operating room. A scrum of medical professionals in a variety of candy-colored scrubs huddled around the table. They reminded me of a box of skittles. Whatever was happening here had already started. But of course it wasn't happening at all. No one moved.

I waited. Nothing.

The possibility that I was still alone nibbled at my brain. Maybe I was still in that hospital bed, racked with a fever, dying, and this was just another hallucination. I went into the OR. Approached the table. I stood next to the anesthesiologist. A nurse was handing a surgeon what looked like a pair of tongs. The guy on the table was cracked open. I could see his heart. Some doctor on the other side of the table had his hand right in there, pressing two fingers against the heart, which of course was not beating. There was no way to know if it had stopped or if it was frozen with the rest of them.

I had never seen the inside of a person. Sure, in movies, people were turned inside out all the time by killing machines. But this was the real deal. All the others around the table were staring as intently at the heart as I was.

Well, almost everyone.

One guy at the end was looking at me. All I could see was his eyes. He couldn't be staring at me. He must have been looking at the place where I was now, where he'd seen something else before. Had to be.

Then, he blinked.

I flinched, stepping backward into a table of instruments. They clattered to the floor. The guy hadn't moved. Just that blink. But maybe I'd imagined it.

Wait. His hand was out in front of him now. Holding a scalpel. And I could swear he was grinning under that mask.

Oh shit. I'm dead. Horror movie time.

"Hey, Duck."

I screamed. Then turned. Then ran. Then crashed into the glass door and fell to the ground. I heard him moving quickly toward me. It was too late. He was on me, holding me down. Laughing.

I recognized that laugh. It couldn't be.

"Carlos?"

"Damn, that was hilarious. Paranoid much?"

It was Carlos.

"How the hell—"

"Look at this, Duck. It's amazing."

Carlos had walked back to the table. He was pointing at the heart.

"The people around this table literally have this guy's life in their hands. He lives or dies because of them. How cool is that? To be that powerful."

Yeah, whatever. I was still trying to process. Carlos was here, not in Uruguay or Colombia or some other South American country.

"Where did you—"

"You know all those stories about how doctors leave things in patients by accident. Maybe this is what happens. The world freezes. And idiots like you and me who aren't frozen put things in there during surgery. When the world unfreezes, whatever we put in there stays because the surgeon doesn't know it's there. What should we put in him? How about a screwdriver?"

This was definitely the kind of shit Carlos would say.

"Are you real?"

Carlos looked right at me. It was the stare he used on girls and teachers and me when he was about to say something serious but he wanted to hypnotize you first. It never failed. He put a hand on my shoulder. I felt it and almost started to cry.

"Duck, of course I'm real."

"You think the world is going to unfreeze?"

I don't know why that's what I asked. But I wanted more than anything right at that moment to hear Carlos' answer.

"Yeah, Duck, I do."

I believed him. Things may suck for me, but not for Carlos. Everything always went his way and I was ready to go along for the ride.

The Frozen Planet's Guide to Washington D.C.

OVERVIEW.
Our nation's capital is a wonderful place to be frozen. A rich history, good food, and plenty of attractions make it one of the premier destinations for tourists in the frozen world. It would probably get really good ratings on Yelp, but unfortunately response rates among the immobile are too low to provide reliable measures of statistical significance.

GETTING THERE AND AROUND.

Washington D.C. is served by three major airports: Dulles, Reagan National, and BWI. None of them are open. There are no flights. You can travel to D.C. by train, arriving at Union Station, just a few blocks from the Capitol. Trains aren't currently running. Go Greyhound—take the bus. Yeah, never mind. If you aren't frozen in D.C., you can walk or ride a bike to get here.

Once you are in the city, there is a world class public transportation system. Remember to call the subway the Metro in order to avoid being pegged as a tourist. Except that the Metro is also frozen so don't bother calling it anything at all. Bike or walk to all your key destinations.

WHEN TO GO AND WEATHER.

You don't really have a choice on that one, now do you? You go whenever you froze. It is 71 degrees and sunny. Always. Unless it isn't. Conditions may vary. (The author of this chapter is starting to wonder if following the section headings from a Lonely Planet guide he picked up at random —Romania, Bulgaria and Albania—may not actually prove to be useful.)

HOTELS.

(Yeah, these section headings are a waste of time.)

Stay in any room you can get into. They are all free.

ATTRACTIONS.

Okay, that one we can work with.

Here are some key sites you won't want to miss on any tour of frozen D.C.

The White House

If you are frozen in the middle of the day, you might actually find the President of the United States engaged in affairs of state. This is pretty exciting, though honestly a frozen president looks a lot like the ones at Madame Tussauds. Seeing frozen famous people is generally weird.

Note that the inside of the White House looks nothing like the set of *The West Wing*. Except for the Oval Office. That's pretty much the same. If you live in D.C., you are likely to have seen this before. It seems like every year, there is at least one kid who has a mother who is a White House correspondent or a father who is an economic advisor or a close family friend who is a secret service agent or a sister who is an intern. All these folks have West Wing tour privileges when the president is out of town. Those tours are pretty sterile and quiet. Normal tourists in the real world can also take the East Wing Tour, but to be honest, to the author that one always felt like waiting in line at a theme park but never actually getting to the ride.

Visiting the White House in your frozen world is different. Technically, you are breaking the law and trespassing. If the world unfreezes while you are in the White House, prepare yourself for lengthy questioning, or depending on your proximity to the President, to be shot. There are two ways to get into the White House. You could scale the fence, which is logistically complicated and potentially dangerous. Or you can jump the turnstile at one of the Secret Service checkpoints.

Your tour should begin at the Oval Office, and if you are lucky, you will find a gaggle of photographers and reporters waiting to go inside for a photo op. A press aide may be holding the door open with one hand and restraining the reporters with the other. Frozen world tourists may go directly inside. It is possible that you will find the president looking bored. There may be a man sitting next to him, also looking bored. Check the schedule on the clipboard of another press aide inside the room.

1:10–1:25: Press availability with president of Argentina.

Congratulations. You are witnessing diplomacy in action. This will be exciting until you realize that literally no one, including the most powerful leader in the free world, has any clue what is going on. This might disturb some people.

Another must-see stop on your White House tour is the press room. Feel free to stand behind the podium and give a speech. It could be this one:

"My fellow Americans, I come to you this afternoon to bring you hope. We are in a time of crisis. We must all stand together. Though you cannot hear me, I know you are listening. Though you cannot move, I know you are doing all you can to maneuver through these troubled times. I want you to know that as the sole representative of the unfrozen human race, I have a plan. It is not a very good plan. And I doubt it will be effective. But it is a plan. And I intend to see it through. So rest easy tonight—I mean, this afternoon. Let me leave you with one final thought. I greatly appreciate that you have placed your faith in me. Unfortunately that was a horrible miscalculation on your part and we are all fucked. Good night and God bless."

The Capitol

Unlike the White House, the U.S. Capitol is easily accessible. You should start your visit in the rotunda. You can climb way up into the dome. Go ahead—no one will stop you.

From there, proceed to the House and Senate Chambers. They both look smaller in reality than on TV. If there is a vote in process, you will have the opportunity to see that most senators and representatives spend a lot of time milling around aimlessly, making small talk in clusters of like-minded legislators and generally acting like awkward teenagers at a school dance during these critical moments that shape the way we all live our lives. Sometimes they play Candy Crush on their phones. Don't be discouraged. That is democracy.

If there is no vote, the chamber will likely be empty with the exception of one representative from one party giving a speech for the C-SPAN cameras and one representative from the other party bored out of his/her mind but unable to leave due to the rules of Congress.

If you climb onto the podium, you might find the Speaker's gavel. Pound away. Call order. Give a speech. It can be the same speech you delivered at the White House, but this time make sure to blame the administration for everything. This is your sacred duty as a member of Congress.

Smithsonian National Zoo

Actually, wherever you are frozen, it is highly recommended that you visit the zoo. Understand that there are major risks in being certain places, such as the gorilla enclosure, in the event the world unfreezes. But if you can get past that fear, you will enjoy the most amazing petting zoo ever.

Highlights at the National Zoo include cuddling a panda bear, riding an elephant (which will require you to find a chair to give you a boost onto the giant animal's back), and hanging out with gibbons.

In the event that you are not alone in your frozen world, beware of dares. These have a tendency to escalate quickly and without restraint—particularly if you are teenagers and your companion is Carlos.

Dares might include, but are not limited to: draping a cobra around your neck, diving into a tank full of piranhas, prying open the mouth of a tiger and sticking your hand inside, slapping a polar bear, and tipping a water buffalo. You might find that your friend Carlos possesses a devious imagination that limits the appeal of this game.

TRAVELING ALONE.

It is most likely that you will be traveling alone in your frozen world. That is unfortunate. There is so much to share. And after a long period of solitude, most people welcome any company they find.

However, if you happen to find yourself traveling with Carlos, be prepared to adjust your expectations. For example, rather than giving a speech in the press room at the White House, you might be required to pretend to be a reporter instead and ask him questions that he will handle gracefully in a tone that will only become more sarcastic as you try to stump him. You might also have to follow him around pretending to be his Secret Service detail. At the Capitol, you may be told that you are the Sergeant-at-arms, whatever that is.

At the zoo, do not be surprised if he encourages you to put a whole tarantula in your mouth, then calls you a pussy when you don't.

Mise-en-scène: White Flint Mall

BEING WITH CARLOS IN the frozen world was a lot like being with Carlos in the regular world. He has always disappeared for periods of time without telling anyone where he was going. The assumption was always that he was doing something more important than you. That did not change in the frozen world. When he wasn't around, I hoped that he was working on a way to unstick the world. After all, he was the superhero and I was just the sidekick. But when he showed up again, he didn't fill me in on his activities. I was grateful that he at least usually had some new ideas about what we should do.

"Let's have some fun," Carlos said.

He's not always very specific and he doesn't always tell me what he has in mind. But I got on my bike and followed him anyway. Like I had any other choice. It felt like years since I'd had someone to talk to. I would have driven off a cliff behind Carlos (though to be fair, I might have done that when the world was moving, so strong are his powers of persuasion).

I hadn't told Carlos where my bike came from—not that he asked. He had found himself a mini-dirt bike. It was the kind of thing that I knew he liked, but would never have been caught dead riding in our old world. This Carlos was a lot less wary of getting his picture taken or embarrassing his family. Most people never thought the other Carlos was skittish that way, but I knew him pretty well. He was always looking over his shoulder even if that made it nearly impossible for anyone to catch him at it.

So of course I just went with it as he started to bike out of the city up Wisconsin Avenue into Maryland. Carlos stayed ahead of me, swerving back and forth, around cars, popping wheelies and hopping on and off the curb. I tried a wheelie or two with my road bike, but never got more than a few centimeters off the ground. Carlos thought that was hilarious.

"This duck can't fly!" he called as he swerved around a woman pushing a stroller on the sidewalk.

Carlos quacked at me and I flipped him a bird of my own. I missed hanging out with him and Grace. We soon fell into a comfortable silence pedaling our way to the 'burbs, and my mind wandered back to Grace. Where had she been frozen? Or was she frozen at all? If Carlos was moving, maybe there was something about the three of us that was special. We were the heroes of this story and as soon as we were all reunited we'd save the world. Seemed doubtful, though, that Grace would be moving and not find me. Somehow I suspected that she'd be a lot better at finding me than I was at finding her. After all, Carlos had found me and I never saw him coming.

I did see him make the turn into the White Flint Mall parking lot. I had gotten pretty far behind so I had to hustle to catch up. I found his bike propped up against the wall outside the entrance to Lord & Taylor. I let mine fall to the ground and rushed in after him.

"Comrades!"

His voice boomed from somewhere above me. I scanned the area and found Carlos standing at the top of the motionless escalator.

"Or should I say, 'Comrade'!"

I laughed. It was hard not to around Carlos.

"The time has come for the great socialist revolutionary experiment extraordinaire. We have all been made equal by recent events. With the exception of two upstanding young men who have been chosen to implement the Politburo's never-ending-year plan. The first step will be the redistribution of wealth!"

This speech was reminiscent of one that Mr. Zimmerman had given toward the end of his Economic History in the 20th century class. We had been talking about communism and particularly governments that had tried to redistribute resources equally, like China and Russia, except of course none of them actually tried to give everyone a share of the pie but instead used the theory of socialism to enrich a small class of oligarchs or plutocrats or whatever that weren't so different from the tsars and emperors they replaced. Basically, Mr. Zimmerman taught me that no matter how pure the theoretical motivations are behind a system of thought, people are going to fuck it up.

Mr. Zimmerman was an earnest man with tiny glasses and a bald head. He wasn't one of the hippy teachers; he seemed more like a tenured professor. But he, like all teachers at LSGC(AWGWU), felt the need to be different and creative in his lesson plan. Maybe the teachers did that because they knew how much money we were paying to be there.

"Empty your wallets. All cash on your desks."

I'll be honest, the kids at LSGC(AWGWU) were usually game for such shenanigans, so you shouldn't be surprised to hear that everyone did what they were told. We were a little surprised when Mr. Zimmerman walked around and took everyone's cash.

"I'm now going to count it up and give everyone an equal share. That's socialism."

That didn't go over too great. I was fine with it because I only had a few bucks on me that day (or any day). But some kids had significant cash with them (as they did every day), and Mr. Zimmerman made a critical mistake by not having anyone count their money before he snagged it. In some ways, he reminded me of my father.

Kids got upset. The principal got involved. Grievances were filed. Mr. Zimmerman took the retirement he was eligible for. Just another day at LSGC(AWGWU).

"Let's begin, shall we?" Carlos was walking down the escalator toward me. I found myself wondering if it was an up or down escalator. Didn't matter now. "Duck, if you'll do the honors."

He pointed to a man standing next to me. The guy was wearing a suit that didn't fit him too well. He must have been in a hurry. It looked like he might have been walking fast in the direction of the perfume counter. Maybe he was taking a late lunch, with only a little time to grab a belated birthday present for his wife. Or possibly an early one for his mistress. Carlos wanted me to do something to him, but I had no idea what.

I finally understood when Carlos got to the bottom of the escalator and started to rifle through a middle-aged woman's purse. He pulled his hand out and showed me the wad of bills.

"Only the cash, Duck," he said, "from everyone."

Whatever you say, man.

Turns out that I'd make a lousy pickpocket. I could see the guy's wallet making a bulge in his back pocket, like a rectangular boil on his ass. But I couldn't manage to pull it out. It was in there good. Finally I had to push from the bottom while yanking from the top to get that sucker free.

All for four dollars. The guy must use a lot of plastic. That's how his wife would catch him.

"You want the credit cards?" I asked Carlos.

"Nah. Just the cash. And it's not for me. Or you. We aren't gonna take a dime." He paused and waved his arms in the general direction of the mall. The dozen or so people I could see ignored us as usual. "We're doing this for the people."

Carlos' plan was grander than I had imagined, but then his plans usually were. He wanted to collect all the money in the entire mall. From every person and cash register. He wanted it all.

I had no idea what we would do with our haul. But I did know that every bill and coin in that sprawling mall needed to be acquired. After that first theft, it became easier, and I started to work more methodically, going through purses, emptying wallets, my fingers probing deep into all the hiding places. Carlos took the first floor of Lord & Taylor; I worked the second. I soon had a big wad of bills and a handful of coins. But I still didn't know what to do with my take.

Carlos returned with a shopping bag full of cash. Smart. I dumped my money in with his.

"To the fountain."

The White Flint Mall has a big fountain in the middle—the centerpiece visible from all the balconies. In December, this is where the giant Christmas tree sits. But all other times of the year, it is barren, a desert of concrete and steel nozzles. Probably broken and too expensive to fix. Or maybe the water bill was too high. Whatever, the management of this mall decided not to turn it on.

It became our money bath. Carlos dumped that first load in, then we divided the mall up by quadrants, by store, person by person, cash register to cash register. We watched it fill up, a sea of green. The paper bills, regardless of denomination, did not stack neatly, but jostled and cramped each other, corners sticking up, faces of dead presidents drowning, so that the bills seemed to be a roiling sea.

"We're not stealing," Carlos said. "We are reinventing society."

I slept and woke many times in that mall, dedicating all my energy to our project. There were long periods where I didn't see Carlos at all. I was working my part of the mall and I assumed he was canvassing his. We would meet occasionally at the fountain, dump in some cash and maybe go get some food together at the food court or Dave & Buster's.

I could spend an afternoon or what felt like one trying to break into a single cash register. The keys were unresponsive, the screens stared blankly at me as all computers maddeningly did. But I found that nearly every drawer popped open if it hit the wall or the floor at the right angle. There were some registers, some safes, that I could not get into. Those pissed me off.

At first I slept on couches in the better stores, but as the fountain filled up, I began to sleep in there with the cash, gathering it all under me as a mattress. I inevitably woke up with my head pressed against a hard nozzle or solid concrete, but it was worth it to drift off feeling rich—no not rich exactly, satisfied, and not because of the amount of money, which was of no use to me or those around me, but because of the steady progression as the fountain filled up, a passage of, yes, time, that I could feel when I lay down atop it, understanding tangibly that the pile was bigger and more comfortable than the last time I had laid down.

Then I woke up and it was over. I retraced my steps through the mall and knew without a doubt that we had all the money. I still didn't know why.

Carlos was nowhere to be found. He always knew things before me, so if I knew we were done, he must have known it too. I checked the food court first. We'd gotten into the habit of having breakfast at the Cinnabon. Nearly all the hot cinnamon rolls on the tray were gone. There were some cold ones in the display case. I had tried one and it wasn't the same.

From the food court, I checked the other places we'd been hanging out when we weren't collecting the cash. He wasn't in Dave & Buster's either. I was pretty hungry so I had a plate of onion rings before continuing my search. D&Bs was probably the most depressing place in the mall. So many games and no way to play them. I could shoot some baskets and whack some moles, but the videogames were all stuck on various scenes of carnage.

I found Carlos in Victoria's Secret. Big surprise there. The floor to ceiling pictures of women in lingerie certainly had a magnetic pull. In the frozen world, you could almost convince yourself that those still photographs were actually live supermodels in the store with you. Nothing else moved; why should they?

Carlos wasn't looking at the posters. He was staring at three girls—our age, possibly a bit older—who all had hangers in hand and were headed toward the dressing rooms.

"If the world had frozen a few minutes later, we'd be having some fun," Carlos said.

His smirk scared me.

I'd been down that road. It didn't go anywhere good.

"What do you want to do with all the money?"

Carlos wasn't in the mood to be distracted.

"We could help them out. They want to try stuff on. That's their intention, right? So what's the harm in doing it for them? Like playing dress up."

I thought about my father and his theories about consequences being relative to the presence of others. That there is no morality unless there is the context of another's judgment.

Now that Carlos was here, we could judge each other.

"I don't think so," I said. "Not as fun as it sounds."

Carlos looked at me. I knew he was disappointed, but he was willing to go along with my decision. For now. He headed toward the door, back out into the mall. But he paused.

"You know we can do anything we want, Duck," he said. "Anything."

He walked away. I followed.

"What are we doing with the money?" I said.

"We already did it. We leave it there."

I could hear the disappointment in Carlos' voice. He wanted something from me. And it wasn't merely to agree to strip down some cute girls. Something deeper. I had no idea what it was, but I suspected when the time came, I'd probably give in.

We left the mall without another word, got on our bikes and headed back into D.C.

Bucket Lists

SOMETIMES YOU DO STUPID stuff with your friends, though my stupid stuff is less stupid than most teenagers.

Grace and I bought lunchboxes. We were walking around Adams Morgan and ducked into one of those funky stores where everything looks shabby but it is expensive because it is old. Grace likes to look around those places. I think it is because her parents are always getting new sleek modern stuff for the house, but her tastes run to more homey and comfortable. Grace's room is like a giant beanbag, all pillows and stuffed animals.

So we were in there, and we never buy anything, except this time Grace stops dead in her tracks and grabs my arm. That's what she does when she really wants my attention. Digs her nails into my bicep.

"We need those," she said.

"Why?" I said.

"Shut up."

Grace took the two lunchboxes off the shelf. One looked like it was a Transformers lunchbox, but on closer examination it was something called the Micronauts. I Googled them later.

They were like these alien robot action figures from the late '70s that were probably really cool when kids didn't have any really cool stuff to play with. Grace handed that one to me. She kept the Strawberry Shortcake one for herself. I looked at the price tag.

"Thirty-five bucks? For a lunchbox."

"It's not a lunchbox," Grace said, walking away to the cash register.

I knew that I was going to buy it. Grace had that look that said she had an idea and if I didn't go along with it she would make me regret it. Luckily, I almost always liked the ideas that followed that look.

We paid. Hers was more than forty bucks. I guess there are more Strawberry Shortcake collectors than Micronauts lovers out there. Or the store just slapped some random numbers on hollow metal boxes as a cultural experiment to see if any idiots would pay for them.

It was a bit embarrassing getting on the Metro with our lunchboxes. They were impossible to hide. Grace opened hers in her lap and felt around the inside as if she was looking for a secret compartment.

"You're not going to make me bring this to school, are you?" Grace laughed.

"This will never leave your bedroom."

Okay. Fine. What the hell?

"It's a time capsule," she said. "We will put things in here for the future."

I said nothing. She wasn't expecting me to. That look.

"And it's an advanced communication device."

Her expression dared me to question that.

"You know how they told us we need to have an emergency plan. A way to contact loved ones in case of disaster."

"Like the zombie apocalypse."

"Or the Rapture. That's what these are for. If you ever have something to tell me, you put it in your lunchbox. I'll know to look there. And I'll do the same."

"How will I know there's something in there? Do we have a bat signal?"

"You'll just know."

And that was that. We went back to my house and made our first deposit in our time capsule/advanced communications systems. Bucket lists. Five things we wanted to do before we died. That list wasn't for an emergency. It was for the future.

Here was mine:

1. Survive high school
2. Lose my virginity
3. Win a Nobel Prize (subject to be determined later)
4. Direct successful indie movie
5. Don't go crazy

Grace wouldn't let me read her list. She thought mine was pretty funny.

My mother taught me a completely different meaning for bucket list. It was a couple months ago (or at least a couple months before the world froze) when she sat me down at the dining room table. She had a bunch of folders neatly lined up in a file box. I knew this was not going to be fun.

"I needed to pull this all together while I'm still lucid," she said. "Things you need to know before I ...."

Die.

The unspoken word echoed in my mind as she started to rustle through the folders. Of course, my mother the archivist had everything cataloged precisely. Whatever emotion was about to push her over the cliff seemed to have receded. I had thought maybe we'd have to do this another time. No such luck.

"Let's start with the money," she said.

My mother took a sheet of paper from a folder labeled "Financial—cash accounts" and slid it in front of me. A list of financial institutions, account numbers, PIN numbers and dollar amounts. It was more than I would have guessed we had.

"Don't lose that one. It pretty much has all someone would need to clean you out."

She laughed, more of a chuckle really, forced. I couldn't take my eyes off the numbers. That's what we were worth.

My mother started with the first line and proceeded to explain every item in excruciating detail. That's how she was.

We plowed through the entire stack of folders. Insurance—life, car, personal items. Something called an *umbrella* policy, which she explained but honestly I couldn't stop picturing that ad about some insurance company that actually uses an umbrella as a logo.

She snapped her fingers in front of my face. "Pay attention. Everything I'm saying is important."

We went over her will and her living will. She showed me the mortgage. One folder contained every company that she used to maintain the house—gutters, AC/heat, roofers, landscapers, painters, and so on. She had researched three realtors in case I wanted to sell the house. There was a list of doctors, dentists, lawyers, and accountants. A folder with everything I needed to know about her job and benefits at GW.

My mind started to wander again as I thought about how long this must have taken to pull together. Snapping fingers brought me back.

It took a few hours, but we went through all her folders. It was exhausting. But it seemed to make her feel better, so I sat through it. I didn't ask any questions. Soon, there were only three folders left. My mother paused. I wasn't sure she wanted to deal with the rest. Maybe we were done.

Nope. She picked up an overstuffed accordion folder.

"This is all the paperwork on your father and St. Elizabeths. Maybe some other things. Names of people involved in the case. I haven't really looked at it in a while. But it's all there."

This was the only folder she didn't take any paper out of; she just moved it onto the completed pile.

Next, we went through her burial arrangements. She'd

picked a funeral home and plots for her and my father in a cemetery. She'd bought a casket. Another list of numbers for everyone who would be involved in the ceremony. It included a retired judge—a friend of hers—who would preside, and a fellow librarian who would handle notifying everyone who needed to be notified.

I picked up another piece of paper. No names or numbers, just prose.

"My obituary," she said. "I didn't want you to have to write that."

That's when I realized that a real bucket list is not the things you want to do before you die, but the things you have to do.

Number 6—write own obituary.

My mother's hands were trembling slightly. She had been getting weaker and weaker. I could see it in the unsteadiness when she walked across the room or reached up to get something out of the pantry. But I knew she was determined to get through this.

There was one more folder. It was labeled "Holidays" and it was empty.

"I don't know why I made this one." She started to cry. "I thought Grace or Carlos might have you for Thanksgiving, maybe the other one for Christmas."

She looked at me for a long moment. I could see her revising her bucket list in her head, moving "Don't die" to number one, knowing that was not an option.

My mother stood up without another word. I heard her climb the stairs and close the door to her room. I gathered all the folders and put them back in the box.

I have a new bucket list:

1. Restart the world
2. Turn 18
3. Lose my virginity
4. Talk to someone (other than Carlos)
5. Don't die

Discussion: Entertainment

A S A PUBLIC SERVICE, the author provides the following options for entertaining yourself in a frozen world. These can be done alone or with a companion. The level of your interest and amusement depends on your temperament and general state of mind.

MOVIES.

You may be surprised to discover that there are movies in your frozen world. Of course, they are all merely single screen shots of whatever was showing at the time of your individual event. Still, the author has included this traditional form of entertainment, though it takes some creativity to enjoy.

One option is to enter the theater and engage in a stream-of-consciousness telling of events in the film that occur following the shot on the screen. This can be a short game focused on what happens immediately after the frozen moment. Or it can be a much longer endeavor if you get on a roll and end up telling yourself the entire movie. This can be done out loud as a performance for the other patrons or silently as a meditative exercise.

If you are at a multi-screen theater, the author recommends a variation on the game in which you start on one screen, begin telling yourself a story, then move to another theater where you need to incorporate that scene into the saga you are spinning. Repeat until finished or bored.

If you have a companion in your frozen world, take a seat in the front row and go all Mystery Science Theater on the shot. The author suggests that this game is best done with a friend who likes your jokes. Otherwise, prepare for awkward pauses because honestly not that many people can rock the necessary improv (or at least that's what Carlos said).

In the interest of keeping a complete record, there will be instances where the screen shot involves an attractive actress and frontal nudity. Pulling a Pee Wee Herman is an option (see *Discussion: Sex*).

People Tipping.

If you happen to be in Iowa or Nebraska or one of those big states in the middle of the country, feel free to engage in a traditional round of cow tipping. It is probably safer when the cow can't get up and stampede over you. Another exotic option is to tip something at your local zoo, like a wallaby or an emu. (The author does not recommend trying to tip something larger, like an elephant or hippo, since you'll probably just pull a muscle or knock yourself out from the failed effort. Those things weigh like a ton and a half.)

In the event that you are unable to find animals to tip, the author will refer to, but not recommend for legal reasons, the practice of people tipping. Note that the author cannot be held responsible for any injuries incurred during such activity that may lead to tort cases in the unfrozen world.

It is easy enough to approach any frozen person, give them a little shove, and watch them fall over. When you are first introduced to the immobile around you, this will seem cruel. You will worry about hurting them. But after some time (or

5

lack of time) you will come to view them more as statues than people. You won't feel their pain.

To increase the level of difficulty, the author (or at least the author's friend who came up with this game) recommends seeking out a crowded sidewalk. Then, run headlong into the throng. The goal is to knock over as many unwitting pedestrians as possible without slowing down. They fall silently, like pins to your human bowling ball. Count the number you knock over and divide by the total number of pedestrians in your path to obtain your percentage tip. Feel free to treat this as a competitive game if you have a companion. Or just compete with yourself to keep life interesting.

Get Drunk.

There are many good reasons to get drunk (and more than a few bad ones). Being the only person moving in a frozen world certainly qualifies (on both counts).

Time to Get Drunk

CARLOS WAS STARTING TO lose it. He stopped sitting down, was always pacing. I couldn't entice him into a round of people tipping, even when it involved a crowded downtown sidewalk full of lobbyists and lawyers. It wasn't like him to lack composure, but I could tell he was getting a little ragged around the edges. I'll admit it made me a bit happy to think that I was handling the situation better than he was.

Actually, I knew I was handling it better when he threw a rock through the window of his house. It was a decorative rock that was almost orange, one of a few hundred that created the border around the Delgados' back patio. I noticed the odd color, which was almost certainly not natural, just before the rock shattered the glass.

"You don't have a key?"

Carlos had picked up a second rock. For a moment, I thought he might throw it at another window, but instead he used it to break off the remaining shards on the one he had taken out.

"Yeah, got a key right here. Just felt like breaking something."

Carlos didn't employ sarcasm often, but when he did, it was pretty devastating. I decided not to point out that he hadn't even tried the doors to see if any were open.

He hadn't been home since the world froze. I didn't really like going home either, but I'd done it. Needed to get some clothes. All my stuff was there.

I realized I was standing on the patio alone. Carlos had bounded through the now glass-free window into one of their many bathrooms. It took me a few tries and a deck chair to follow him.

The Delgado house is not as palatial as Mackenzie's mansion, but there is less space in Georgetown than Foxhall. Trade-offs of the Rich and Famous. Still, they managed to have plenty of room. I found Carlos in the cavernous foyer under the crystal chandelier, looking up the stairs to the second floor, where you could stand on a balcony and survey the scene below.

Halfway up the gently curving staircase was an unceremoniously discarded man's dress shirt. A few stairs past that, a woman's skirt. Then, one red high-heeled shoe and a belt that was not immediately identifiable as belonging to a particular gender.

Carlos did not move. For a moment, I thought maybe he had finally succumbed and become frozen. But I could hear him breathing.

Mr. and Mrs. Delgado always seemed happy the few times I saw them together. Lots of incidental touching and meaningful looks. Stuff I never saw at home. Kind of what I thought love should look like.

I didn't think either of them would be cheaters, but this is Washington D.C., where everyone wants you to see want they want you to see, truth be damned. The truth here was that two people were upstairs without most of their clothing, which they had been in a hurry to shed.

Carlos started up the stairs, taking two at a time. I had to jog to keep up with him. The trail of clothing led down a long hallway past rooms previously occupied by Carlos' three sisters. I was hoping that maybe the trail would lead to one of their bedrooms, but no such luck. By the time we got to the bra and panties and briefs, we were approaching the doorway to the bedroom of Carlos' parents.

"You don't need to go in there," I said, putting a hand on his arm.

"I need to know," he said, shrugging me off.

Did I mention that everyone in the Delgado family is gorgeous? I didn't really understand the extent of their perfection until I saw his mother riding his father reverse cowgirl on that king-size bed. I mean seriously, it was perfectly lit, on top of the covers, fully flexed and exposed, like some ridiculous porno screen shot. They both even had their backs arched and their lips forming a perfect simultaneous moan. Carlos' parents were toned and built and stacked and buff and *damn,* I had to look at the wall to avoid getting a hard on, and then I had to look at another wall where there wasn't a mirror because somehow the reflection made the whole thing even more of a turn-on.

There is nothing nastier that finding your friends' parents attractive. I know this. I'm sorry.

Carlos turned and stormed out of the room. I thought maybe he'd be relieved that it wasn't an affair, but I guess no kid wants to see their parents like that. Even if their parents are fucking beautiful or I should say beautiful fucking. Okay, I've got to stop now.

I'll admit to taking one last look before following him downstairs. As I stepped around the clothing again, I couldn't help but wonder if it was always the case that this many people I knew were having sex in the afternoon.

Carlos was in the kitchen. Take a minute to appreciate this kitchen. The island was the size of my bedroom. Every appliance was state of the art. I counted at least four stoves, though one might have been a wine refrigerator and I believe I once heard one of Carlos' sisters call another one a "crisper." I pulled out a stool and sat down. Carlos walked over to the refrigerator, which took a while to get to, and started getting out food. The Delgados have a chef who comes in a couple times a week; they always have awesome leftovers. They were so good, you didn't even need to heat them up. I was digging into a piece of cold lasagna when Carlos put a glass in front of me and filled it with Scotch. He did the same with his glass and downed it immediately. Filled it right back up.

Now the thing is that Carlos rarely drinks. Or at least not in public. Based on how he knocked the Scotch back, I started to suspect this was something he did regularly at home. The not drinking in public was more of a defense mechanism of a child of semi-famous people who would be embarrassed by their son making the news. Of course, for most kids in his situation, the drinking in private was also a defense mechanism.

Carlos motioned for me to drink with him. I took a sip. It burned like hell.

"It's worse than I thought," he said.

"It's not like they're having an affair."

I thought I was being helpful. Carlos stared me down.

"Didn't think they were."

He downed another glass of Scotch and refilled immediately. And it dawned on me why we were there. Carlos had been hoping his parents weren't frozen. Been there, done that. That's why I went to St. Es looking for my dad. Hoping our parents might have the answers. Nothing worse for a kid than that moment when you realize they don't know anything more than you do. Of course, Carlos got to visit his folks in a hardcore version of an *Architectural Digest* spread while mine were respectively in a mental hospital and a hearse. So he was still winning.

"It's up to us, Duck," Carlos said. "If we don't solve this, no one will."

There it was. The official call to arms. I finished my drink.

Save Her

AND THAT WAS HOW I ended up back at the Natural History Museum holding a gun to the temple of the man who Carlos and I had definitively decided was a pedophile.

Wait, I skipped a few things. It's all a bit jumbled in this period. That Scotch back at Carlos' was the beginning of an extended period of inebriation (interspersed with intense bouts of vomiting).

I'll try to piece it together. Call these flashbacks ... though that presents an interesting philosophical question. Is a flashback even possible in a world where time has stopped? If everything is happening at the same moment, then nothing can be in the past and there can be no flashbacks.

Oh, screw it. Flashback.

As usual, it was all Carlos' fault. In his kitchen, he demanded that we both meticulously describe everything that had happened since the world froze. He was looking for clues. I was already buzzed, so I missed pretty much all his story. But what I caught was lyrical and magical, a trek of more than 5,000 miles overland, through jungles and cities, a complete epic tour of the Americas told with a grace and wonder befitting a Gabriel

García Márquez novel. I think I slept through most of it.

"Now you, Duck. Spill it."

I squinted, trying to focus. I must have tapped my glass because he filled it up. And then I just got verbal diarrhea and did as he asked. It was like I was floating above myself, watching someone else tell the most ridiculous story ever. On and on it went. Everything that had happened.

When I was done, Carlos was smiling. It was that smile he has when he knows what to do and he knows he's going to be able to convince everyone around him to do it with him.

"Save her," he said.

I burped. It was nasty. Like evaporated puke. That should have been a warning to stop drinking. It didn't take.

"Huh?" That was the syllable I tried to say. It probably was not that clear.

"Your dad gave us the answer. The world froze because someone needs to be saved. A woman or a girl. A 'her.' "

"Uh-huh."

Another burp. Worse this time.

"It must be someone you know. Or someone you've come across recently. I bet you know who you need to save. Just think."

I tried to think. It hurt. Everything was starting to hurt.

The only woman I could think of that needed saving was my mom. And it was too late. She was dead. I wondered if we should go to the hearse and open the coffin and listen for a heartbeat. Then I wasn't sure if they had put her in a coffin or if it was a body bag or if it was even a hearse or maybe an ambulance to take her to the funeral home. The thinking was making me dizzy. Pretty sure it was a hearse. Even if we found her though, her heart would be frozen. Wouldn't be able to hear a pulse. There would be no way to know if they had accidentally declared her dead or if she was actually dead. I was pretty sure she was actually dead and wasn't the one to save. But I couldn't think of anyone else and Carlos was looking at me.

I had to throw up.

Carlos' house has seven bathrooms. There's always one close by.

As I was barfing into the nearest toilet, I knew who we needed to save. The nausea was the same I'd felt looking at the guy staring at the girl who was peering into the geode. I wiped my mouth with toilet paper and slumped back against the wall.

"It's the girl at the museum."

Then I passed out.

I woke up on the floor of the bathroom, staring into the muzzle of the gun lying there in front of my face.

"My parents keep that around in case we get a break-in. Georgetown is not the safest place in D.C., you know."

I might have nodded. I managed to move my arm enough to push the gun so it pointed at the wall instead of my eyeball. Carlos put a beer in front of me. He might as well have hit me over the head with it.

"Let's go to the museum. I hope you remember which one."

RIDING A BIKE WHILE drunk is a stupid thing to do.

It took us a long time to get downtown. I would ride straight for a block or so and then find myself veering off one way or another. I couldn't stop and the momentum inevitably took me into a parked car (or a car that was effectively parked by the frozen world) or over a curb or into a sign post. I'd fall onto the hood of the car or just slump forward on my handlebars. Then I'd stay like that for a little while to recover before remounting and doing it all again.

Carlos thought it was hilarious.

I didn't understand why he wasn't more unstable. He had seemed to match me drink for drink. Maybe one of the reasons I was so shaky was that I was holding a beer the entire ride. When I finished one, Carlos handed me another. I have no idea where he was getting them from.

At least once during the ride, I stopped and took a nap in the middle of the street. Maybe twice.

"Just pull the trigger. Do it. You know what he is."

My hand felt weightless. The heavy gun was the only thing keeping it from floating away.

When we got to the museum, we went through the guy's pockets. (Well, first we went to an exhibit of awesome nature photography because Carlos hadn't seen it yet, and it was pretty cool and made me at least a little bit more sober, but not enough really.)

Here's what the creep had on him:

1. Seven rabbit's feet—two purple, one red, one blue and four pink.

2. A crinkly cheap cellophane bag of individually wrapped primary-colored hard candy. The package label said twelve pieces. There were only eleven left.

3. A knife about four inches long that looked like it might be for hunting, but what the hell did I know about hunting.

Here's what he didn't have:

1. A wallet.

2. Identification.

We laid his belongings on the floor and considered the implications.

What had happened to the one piece of candy that was missing? Did he give it away or did he have a sweet tooth? Was there a girl locked in a basement somewhere who was silently promising never to eat candy again? I hadn't read the news or turned on the TV for weeks before the world froze. As my mother declined into her own white noise, I followed her willingly. It is easy to blame my disappearance on the intensity of her needs, the complete obsessive nature of terminal illness, but that would not be true. I had help—hospice nurses, all paid for by her insurance. Truth is, I had long been predisposed to unplug myself from human interaction, and watching my mother fade away was more than enough excuse for me. But there in the Natural History Museum, I wished that I had been keeping up with current events. Maybe there was a missing girl on the news. I would have known her name. I would know what to look for.

What I did know was that this knife had no real purpose in a museum. I wondered how he had gotten past the metal detectors. Didn't really matter. Here it was.

Despite the haze of the alcohol, which had been augmented by about half a dozen small bottles of wine we had found in the museum cafeteria, I could see in this man's face that he was evil. This was it. The moment to change the world.

I would save *her*.

Carlos nodded his approval.

I pulled the trigger.

Nothing happened.

Of course it didn't. There are no sparks in this world. No way to fire a gun. (See: *Discussion: Machines*.) Carlos looked at me with a massive amount of disappointment and just a touch of pure rage. The world was still frozen.

The nausea didn't surprise me. I'd been feeling that since we got to the museum. It was the shooting pain in my gut that doubled me over and caused me to vomit on the pedophile's shoes and pants. I fell to my knees and started retching again. I wanted to get to a bathroom, but I toppled onto my side, my guts contracting like an accordion played poorly. More, this time spreading out into a pool directly in front of my face. I forced myself to scoot back on the floor to avoid breathing in my own puke. But that just intensified the cramping. I screamed or cried, probably both.

"Pussy!"

My eyes were closed. I didn't know who said it. It had to be Carlos, but it didn't sound like his voice.

"I shot him," I said, though I'm not sure I said it out loud. "The gun doesn't work."

"You don't have the balls for the job. You knew that gun wouldn't work."

Definitely didn't sound like Carlos. Higher pitched. Female. Maybe he was messing with me.

I forced my eyes open. The pain had dulled to a roar instead of a shriek. Nothing had changed. The girl and the geode. The mom and the little boy. The man staring at the girl. Carlos stood behind me. He shrugged. Didn't look too concerned that his friend was doubled up on the ground clutching his gut.

"What did you say?" I toughed out the words.

"I didn't say anything."

"You're gonna pay to dry clean these pants."

It was the pedophile. He hadn't moved. Not a quiver of his lips. But it was his voice. I could feel him smirking at me.

"And then I'm gonna wear them when I go to her room and mess 'em up again."

The voice was behind me, inside me. This was not good. But it was as real as anything I had experienced since the world froze. Another voice chimed in, farther away, small and delicate, sounding so different than it had a few minutes before when calling me a "pussy."

"Save me."

And then the knife was in my hand. Despite the shooting pain in my stomach, I lunged. The motion threw me off balance and the world was spinning. I couldn't keep my feet under me. And as I was falling, I felt my grip on the knife loosening. I wasn't going to stab him. I didn't even know how to stab someone. There will be another way. Until suddenly, the knife caught on something—someone—and was wrenched from my hand as I kept twisting away. I was flying, floating, and then abruptly I wasn't. My head hit the hard floor.

The last thing I thought before there was nothing:

I will save you.

The tiny voice responded:

Thank you.

You're Welcome?

I WOKE UP WITH a splitting headache, a pounding in my ears. My stomach felt like it was in a vice, but at the same time I knew the worst had passed. Whether it was the alcohol or the guilt or something I ate, I'll never know. The vomit was drying, caked on my clothes. I had slept for a long time.

"Duck, you need help," Carlos said. "You stabbed that guy."

Oh crap. I stabbed someone.

I was lying on my back, looking up at the man who might or might not be a pedophile. Carlos was sitting next to me, criss-cross applesauce style, just like we used to on the sharing rug in class when I first met him. So long ago. A different life.

Where had I stabbed him? I remembered feeling the knife catch and jerk away. Now I knew it had lodged in the man's flesh somewhere. Peering up, I checked his head first, hoping I hadn't got him in the eye. No knife there. My eyes scanned his torso, looking for wounds that would have hit his heart or lungs. Nope.

"Lower, Duck," Carlos said.

Oh dear lord, tell me I didn't castrate the guy. Thankfully, no knife to the crotch here. Or to the thighs where I could have severed a femoral artery. I was starting to wonder if Carlos was just messing with me.

"Lower."

I rolled onto my side and there it was. The knife stuck out of the intersection of his ankle and foot at a perfect forty-five degree angle. No blood.

"I stabbed him."

"Yeah, but you did a pretty piss poor job of it."

I stabbed someone in the foot.

"I was hearing voices," I said. "The guy. The little girl."

I pulled myself into a seated position and took a moment to catch my breath from the effort. Everything was the same. No one had moved.

"Yeah, I figured," Carlos said. "Seeing things too."

Wait, what? Oh crap. It was worse than I thought.

"Like you?"

"Yeah, like me," Carlos said.

"So, you're my Tyler Durden."

We'd read *Fight Club* in Mr. Lorenzo's Anarchy in Modern American Fiction class.

"Actually, I think that I'm more Gollum to your Sméagol."

And *Lord of the Rings* in Ms. Tutwell's Geography of Fictional Lands seminar, which somehow got me Social Studies credit.

Damn, I went to a really questionable high school.

But that wasn't the point right then. The point right then was that I was not only hearing voices and seeing people, but my situation had driven me so far around the bend that I was continuing to have a conversation with one of my hallucinations, who was also one of my best friends, except that he wasn't because my friend really was on some do-gooder summer job in Ecuador or Peru or Lothlórien. Who the hell knew?

"And now you're going to go away and leave me here with this guy who is probably not a pedophile with a knife in his foot that I put there?"

"Well, not sure how much credit I give you for the stabbing. More of an inadvertent assist to gravity. But otherwise pretty good summary, Duck."

"Thanks."

"So I have just a few things to say before I go and leave you to save all of us."

Great, shoot.

"Just because the world gives up on you doesn't mean that you give up on the world."

Easy to say when you've got a stable family including stunningly good-looking parents who meet up in the early afternoon to have sex. I really needed to stop thinking about that.

"You can't freeze the world to get away from your problems. You have to face them."

Except that everyone I need dies or gets institutionalized or is a hallucination.

"You can't stay a kid forever. You have to grow up and deal with your lot in life."

These platitudes were getting boring. *If you didn't notice, the world chose to freeze me at seventeen so I would never be an adult.*

"Check the lunchbox."

Blah, blah, blah … wait, that last one was interesting.

Carlos was gone. He was never there. I was alone again, just like I always was.

Except I wasn't alone. There was a guy who'd been stabbed. Looking at the knife, sticking out of his foot like a novelty push pin, I started to laugh. I hadn't saved anyone. Was this all a test? If so, how many times had I failed? Why have a test if the person being tested cannot pass? I thought I'd done everything asked of me. I had accepted this world. I had figured out how to survive within it. I had learned my lessons, all of our lessons. This should be the moment where the world churns back to life. But what if it was just an endless string of tests, no single exam meaning anything more than the previous one or the next one. No answer key. No bell curve. No resolution.

The volume of my breathing gradually increased, a rush of wind in the tunnels in my head, roaring, swelling. This wasn't laughter. I was hyperventilating. Everything rushed down on me. Wheezing filled my head. My cheeks were wet, but I didn't know if it was tears or sweat. My body convulsed. "This is the way it ends," I said in a disembodied voice. I was watching myself destruct. Cowardly. A whimper not a bang. Unobserved.

Discussion: Suicide

THE AUTHOR WOULD LIKE to point out that lots of people think about suicide. It seems like an easy answer when things are tough. But of course it isn't easy at all. Making yourself do something that will kill you goes against all our survival instincts. Even swallowing handfuls of pills while telling yourself that you're just eating candy doesn't really work because our brains know the reality. It is very hard to lie to ourselves convincingly.

Grace's brother hung himself in his room. Grace found him. He was a smart guy, a bit of an introvert, who spent a lot of time in MMPGs, making friends with real people who could only communicate with him through avatars. No one knows why he killed himself. He didn't leave a note. He gave no warning. But he had been thinking about it for a while. Long enough to learn how to tie a real noose. Seriously, that's hardcore shit when you're not just going to use a belt, but actually go find the thick rope and learn how to tie it and then follow through.

In your frozen world, you will have plenty of time to be that methodical. You can take as much time as you need to learn the skills you need to engage in a proper suicide. But what might ultimately stop you is the fact that it bugs you that probably no one will ever find your body.

Mise-en-scène: Grace's House

I DON'T KNOW WHEN it started exactly, but it was the custom at LSGC(AWGWU) for boyfriends and girlfriends to write letters to each other. It was a statement on the relationship when one or the other broke the ice by putting pen to paper. He or she was saying this was more than ephemeral, more than transitory, more than any number of other SAT words we'd memorized. A letter confirmed that what you were feeling was real.

Yeah, I know, if you happen to be an adult reading this in your own frozen world, you're calling bullshit right now. You think teenagers don't know how to write, let alone communicate through the arcane art of exchanging letters, what with all the texting acronyms and contractions and whatnot. Well, get over yourself. It's not exactly discovering cold fusion. Yes, we can craft a complete sentence. All that other stuff is for one simple purpose—to keep you from knowing what we're talking about.

But I digress. I didn't write any letters, never really had the opportunity. A couple of times I started ones to Mackenzie, but I knew it was wrong. This was not a casual undertaking. And you never wrote a letter that you knew wouldn't be well received. You only wrote them to someone you trusted intimately and completely.

Mackenzie had plenty of letters from other guys. Sometimes she'd read them in front of me, but never to me. Carlos had letters too. He never shared them with me either. Some things are still private.

Love letters and suicide notes deserve to be written in ink.

I walked to Grace's house. When I left the museum, I couldn't find my bike and I didn't feel like stealing another one. Besides, I needed the walk to clear my head. Needed to slough off the drunkenness and the lingering malaise from my first felony assault. None of it seemed real. And now that "Carlos" had revealed himself and disappeared, I was seriously questioning everything. I had basically run out of things to do. But I was still here.

I had one lead on a purpose in life and it was given to me by my own hallucination. Not exactly a firm foundation to set a life goal on. But I was going to go check the lunchbox because what else was I going to do and I was more than a little scared about what would happen when I really couldn't think of anything else to do.

I got to Grace's street and starting running through the most likely scenarios. First, I open the lunchbox and find the same stuff that I already know is in there. It doesn't help at all and there's nothing else to do. Second, Grace is sitting in her bedroom waiting for me. She moves. I was pretty sure that if that happened it would mean I was seeing things again. But I wasn't sure if I cared. I'd really liked having company. I supposed a third option would be that I wouldn't be able to find her lunchbox. That would suck.

Here's what actually happened. The front door was wide open. That I didn't expect, but it made life a little easier.

Grace's dad was inside, just a couple of steps into the foyer. He had his cellphone pressed against the side of his head and was listening intently. I could see where the corner of his phone was going to leave an indentation next to his temple. His entire face was creased with concern. Seriously, everywhere there could be a wrinkle, he had one, deep and furrowed.

I went upstairs to Grace's room. Her mom was already in there, sitting at Grace's desk, fingers poised above the keyboard. Grace's email was open. It was the account she used only for online registrations, but her parents probably didn't know that. Grace's mom's face was also lined and intent. She had been looking for an answer to some question. I had no idea what it was, but it must have been pretty important. I felt bad that we were so good at hiding things from our parents. They really didn't have a chance of finding what they were looking for.

In the middle of the afternoon. On a work day.

There was a scrap of paper next to the keyboard.

"Dr. Klein. Nat. Hist. Looking for Grace. Didn't come in today."

Then a phone number that I couldn't call.

Suddenly that Strawberry Shortcake lunchbox was much more intriguing. I went into Grace's closet. She kept a retractable stepstool in the back corner. I opened it up and got on the top step. My hand snaked through the museum of no-longer-worn sweaters that occupied the uppermost shelf. Back behind the soft façade, my fingers found the hard metal lunchbox. I brought it down.

Sitting on her bed, I ran my fingers over Custard, Strawberry Shortcake's cat, from head to tail. Grace always petted the cat before she opened the box as if it were some secret lock. I wasn't taking any chances.

Most of the things in the lunchbox, which was stuffed to capacity, were familiar to me. The bucket list. Various ticket stubs and the playbill from when we went to see *Book of Mormon*. Boarding passes and pictures. Lots of time capsule material. Top ten lists. I was overwhelmed by the realization that so much of what was important to Grace, so much of what she had done in the past few years, involved me. Guilt followed. I had stood her up for prom and checked out on her completely in the months leading up to graduation. I had to force myself to believe that it wasn't too late.

There were two envelopes in the lunchbox I had never seen before. One, thick, was full of paper. Grace had written "Carlos" on that one. The other was thin—that one said "Duck." Both envelopes were sealed. For the addressees' eyes only.

I slipped my finger under the corner of my envelope and ripped. For a fleeting moment, I wondered if it was a love letter. Turned out it was the next worst thing. A suicide note.

Grace's Note

GRACE ALWAYS SAID THAT if she wrote a suicide note it would be a grace note. She tried to make it funny, but neither of us could laugh. I always told her to stop saying things like that and I was dead serious.

Here's what her note said:

> Duck,
> It's not your fault.
> Please tell Carlos it isn't his fault either. Make sure he gets the envelope with his letters. Tell my parents there was nothing they could do. Maybe we're just all wired this way. I don't know. Tell my sister that she can be different.
> I went to the cabin in West Virginia.
> I'm sorry,
> *Grace*

Fuck.

Home and Hearse

For the first time since the world froze, I was hoping it would not start up again before I was ready. And I wouldn't be ready until I managed to get to West Virginia and find Grace.

Luckily I had a map. And Google directions to her cabin. Grace made me print them out and put them in my Micronauts lunchbox. It was part of our preparation for the zombie apocalypse. Everyone knows that the electrical grid would collapse when the dead rose from the earth. We were going to meet up at the cabin. It's not like we expected to survive—no one survives the zombie apocalypse—but at least we'd live long enough to have sex and not die virgins. 'Cause nobody wants to die a virgin.

This meant I had to go home. I had only been home a few times since the world froze, mainly in the first days after it happened. I went there to pick up supplies, and I hoped I would get a little comfort. But soon I realized that anything available in my house was readily mine elsewhere throughout the city. There was also no comfort there. Just the empty hospital bed. The smell of industrial disinfectants. The memories of my mother dying. In that house, it was all a fresh wound, whereas in the rest of my frozen world, it was a gash that had long ago scabbed over. Not gone, but healing.

Still, the lunchbox was there, so I had to go home.

It was a long walk and I had only made it to Nebraska Avenue when I saw the man and his son at the playground. The two of them sat at a picnic table having a lunch of crustless peanut butter and jelly sandwiches, baby carrots and Oreo cookies. They had a bike that looked sturdy, built for long distances. But it was the kid carrier attached to it that was the main appeal. I had to get to West Virginia with some supplies, and hopefully back with Grace.

I rode off on my new bike, leaving the father and son side by side, contentedly enjoying the beautiful day. For a fleeting moment, I tried to come up with a comparable moment with my dad. Nothing. Pushed the thought aside—no real use to it. With no child carrier for the boy, they would have to find another way home. But they would be okay. They had each other.

The rest of the trip home went by fast. I was a bit wobbly as I learned to manage the turns with the carrier, but soon I had it down and was pulling into my driveway. I had forgotten the main reason that I didn't go home much.

The hearse was still in the driveway. I hurried inside.

The hospice nurse was there, just as she had always been, in the living room, gathering up supplies to take to someone else's dying relative. I had forgotten about her too.

SO LONG AGO.

I felt the warmth of her hand through my shirt, gentle but insistent, as she held my shoulder and shook me awake. Like all the hospice nurses, she had a kindly face. I was embarrassed that I didn't remember her name, but too close to sleep to hide it.

"I'm sorry, Jacob," she said. "She's gone."

I tried to focus, but the world was still blurry. I was sitting in the chair in the corner. That's where I had fallen asleep around 4 a.m. They had told me it would happen that night. I didn't want to be awake for the end, but I felt I had to try. So I paced the room for hours, listening to my mother's phlegmy breaths, each one a heroic struggle. The nurse did not say a word to me. It was her job to help my mother die and to let me be. Finally, I couldn't stay on my feet. I sat down in the chair and drifted off as the nurse stroked my mother's hair and sang a lullaby softly into her ear in a language I didn't understand.

Now, the gentle kindly insistent nameless nurse knelt before me. I looked past her at the clock. It was 10:37 a.m. this morning.

"You take a moment, honey, okay? Then we'll talk through some things."

I heard her in the first floor bathroom. The nurses used it as a makeshift supply closet, and each sound was magnified as she packed things up—pills my mother had long since been unable to swallow rattling in half-empty plastic bottles, ointments and salves in tubes and jars, unused needles clinking together like champagne glasses.

Looking down at my mother in bed, I wondered how long she had been dead. Though the sheets around her head were soaked through, my mother's cheeks and forehead were dry, all the tangles of hair that had been stuck there through the long night brushed back and tucked neatly behind her ears. The nurse had folded her hands over her stomach and closed her eyelids, creating an appearance of peaceful repose. Then she had awoken me.

I smelled coffee in the kitchen. I was drawn to it. The nurse placed a steaming mug in front of me. I grasped it with both hands, letting the pain focus me.

"Today's gonna be a long day," she said. "You just take it one step at a time. Do you want me to call the funeral home?"

I must have nodded because she went right to the sheet of

paper my mother had printed months earlier that had all the key information on it. It had felt surreal to have your own mother tell you how to dispose of her, and it felt no different at that moment in the kitchen watching a stranger dial the phone and request a transport for the body.

Time passed. Someone else from the hospice arrived, a burly man who loaded one piece of equipment onto a truck then left. The nurse and I sat there waiting for the funeral home, mostly in silence, occasionally punctuated by her questions.

"Are you sure you're not hungry?"

"Is there someone you'd like me to call?"

"Would you like something to help you sleep?"

Through the kitchen window, I saw the hearse back into the driveway. Passersby stopped to stare. Two men clattered a gurney out the back hatch and headed for my front door.

The nurse let them in. I didn't move. The gurney rumbled past in the hallway. I heard the nurse whispering to the men. Then she whispered to me, "Would you like to say goodbye before they take her?"

I didn't realize she was standing next to me. Somehow I managed to shake my head.

"She was wearing this. I thought you would want it."

My mother's necklace hung in front of me, the three interlocking rings swaying pendulous and hypnotic. Finally, I found my voice.

"Give it back to her. It's not mine."

MY LUNCHBOX WAS EXACTLY where it should be, tucked away in the top corner of my closet. Everything that was supposed to be in there was there. Nothing new or surprising. I took out the map and directions. I emptied my backpack of the school books I hadn't looked at in weeks. Those didn't matter anymore. I had graduated—or at least I was pretty sure I had graduated. There would be new books if the world ever started again.

There was a roll of duct tape in the lunchbox. Grace had given it to me as a birthday gift when I turned fifteen. She said I'd need it for the zombies. Duct tape was on the Homeland Security emergency preparedness list, after all. I threw the tape in the backpack. Tossed in a couple of changes of clothes too. I had no idea how long this would take me.

In the bathroom, I packed a toothbrush, toothpaste, and some deodorant. I hadn't been that diligent about my hygiene. If I did find Grace moving, she would give me a hard time about that. Downstairs, in the kitchen, I packed some snacks.

I didn't realize that I needed one more thing until I was outside.

The hearse was unlocked. I swung open the back door. And there she was. I could smell her perfume—the nurse must have dabbed it on her wrists just before they loaded her into the hearse. There was room next to her and I fit myself into that space. For the record, there was no coffin or body bag. She just lay on the gurney with a sheet over her. I pulled it back off her face. I held onto her and I cried.

"Goodbye," I whispered.

Her cheek felt cold against my lips. I reached behind her neck, which had only just begun to stiffen. Finding the clasp, I set free the necklace that had been given to her by my father. I knelt before her, in that cramped space, and put it around my own neck.

What I'd said to the hospice nurse was wrong. This necklace is mine. It is a part of me. My legacy. In exchange, I took off my father's watch. Gently, I clasped it to her wrist.

I closed the back hatch of the hearse behind me.

I was ready to go.

Road Trip

I'LL READILY ADMIT TO having only a high-school level knowledge of existentialism.

Things suck. Nothing happens. There is no hope.

Wait for someone who never shows up. Get locked in a room with no door. Become nauseous at the thought of living.

You probably need to be French to really get it.

My mom sat me down once with a serious look. For most kids, this would probably be when you get the sex talk. She wanted to talk to me about reading existentialism.

"It's something you have to do, but don't take it too seriously. Those books are like bottomless pits. Don't get too close to the edge. You may never climb out."

Maybe you don't have to be French to understand the danger of despair. I was thinking about that as I started on my seventy-mile bike ride from Washington D.C. to Shepherdstown, WV.

I was humming "Road to Nowhere," my mom's favorite Talking Heads song, which is a hell of a lot cheerier than Sartre and Beckett even if it is about going somewhere and nowhere at the same time. It was 71 degrees and sunny. I was feeling pretty good.

I barely made it out of town.

Let me now stress the importance of maintaining an exercise routine in your frozen world. You never know when you might need to run away from something or lift heavy objects or climb out of a deep hole. Or take a long bike trip to West Virginia.

There are mile markers on every highway. Tiny posted signs that tick off the distance by the tenth of a mile. There's probably a law requiring them. Barely noticeable to the cars firing by at sixty, seventy, eighty miles an hour. But on a bike, dragging that damn kid carrier filled with bottled water and snacks behind me, I was intimately aware of each one of them. As I headed out of D.C. on I-270, they mocked me. I felt myself slowing down, each marker taking longer and longer to arrive. Sometimes, I could see the next one out in the distance, running away from me faster than I could pedal.

Only seven miles into my journey, I collapsed by the side of the road in a bed of weeds that looked like wildflowers. I wasn't sure I was going to make it. I stayed there, staring up at the perfect blue sky for a few moments, until I had to roll over and throw up.

I realized that even though I had been biking around D.C., it was mainly in short bursts and often with frequent coasting.

But I had to keep going for Grace. I got back on the bike.

Any notion of speed became inconsequential. Useless. Miles per hour. Feet per second. Fine lot of help those are. You need time to make those relevant. The bike I stole had an odometer. That's what it said on the plastic casing that held the LED readout. I could see the wires snaking down the frame to the wheel. But it wouldn't turn on or tell me anything about my progress.

I counted the revolutions of the wheels as I pushed forward. There were times as I biked that I felt as if I wasn't moving. That all my effort, the tensing and relaxing of my muscles, the pumping of my legs and the strain in my back, was an illusion. Everyone else was moving—all these cars and trucks I passed on the road—and I was stationary. Ticking off the rotations prevented me from believing I was going nowhere. (And of course that Talking Heads song, which I happen to love as much as my mom did, was now stuck in my head playing on an infinite loop to mock me.)

But I was going nowhere. And I knew nothing. Everything I had done had been wrong. And all of my ideas about what to do next were convoluted and contradictory. There was no logic governing my next act. No strategy for my next move. It had all become random and so I found myself on someone else's bike dragging a kid carrier filled with junk food and water, riding to West Virginia.

What if I got to Grace's cabin and she was already dead?

This thought made me bike faster. The brief fleeting moments where I could shut off my brain by the simple hypnosis of spinning tires were not enough to banish these dark thoughts that had overtaken me.

Save her.

Maybe she needed to save *me*.

It was all coming back to me now. That emptiness, that despair, that I realized had disappeared when the world froze. The gnawing ache of loneliness that had descended on me, that had taken root long before, when my father had been institutionalized, when my mother had gotten sick, when I felt Mackenzie had cheated on me even though we weren't even dating, now returned. It seemed ridiculous, laughable, that I stopped being lonely only at the moment when I was truly alone. But that was what had happened when the rest of the world stopped and I kept moving. I had shed all that happened before like snakeskin, not the trappings of my life, but the emotions tangled up in it. I had let go and been engulfed by the new reality.

I had decided to continue living.

But as I rode toward West Virginia, I remembered why I had wanted to die.

Everyone has thought about suicide. I told you that already.

The air grew thick. There was a shift in the temperature, anticipatory. The weather in D.C. had been constant, but I was too spun up, too wrapped in my own troubled mind, to enjoy the change in climate. By moving, I had forced the world's hand and made it admit that not everything was the same. In the distance I could see the downpour, sheets of water hanging from the dark clouds like curtains of cellophane waiting to flutter to the ground and wrap the Earth. A fierce thunderstorm. I hurtled toward it. To the West, I could see a single lightning strike, cleaving the sky in two. It looked like a zipper, hanging there, and I wondered what waited on the other side if it was ever undone. I stared at the lightning for a long time; the road before me seemed to wind toward it. I waited for it to dissipate, knowing it never would, that it would forever be there, licking the charred soil with its crackling tongue.

The storm refused to come to me, so I raced toward it. I had to laugh at the pathetic fallacy of it all, even as the darkening sky cast a shadow over my turbulent thoughts.

The sheets of rain were closer than I thought, and soon I was riding through the water, which coated my face like a mist and fell to the ground behind me, blackening the highway. I cut a swath through the storm. Where I had been there was now an absence, a long smudge. The water hung above and around it. But the path I had taken was dry. Like an eraser, I had wiped away a layer of chalk dust and left an empty space on the board for someone else to fill in.

I got off my bike, running in circles around it. Poking my hands, my arms, my legs, my head into the water, making the rain fall. I was a child and the world was my Etch A Sketch. I erased the rain with a shake of my hand. I wrote my name in the sky. I drew pictures. The wonder of it distracted me from my thoughts. But only for a moment.

I knew my goal was the lightning. I could still see it in the distance, but not far, fuzzy through the gauzy layers of water around me. It looked like it struck somewhere just beyond a nearby farmhouse.

I abandoned my bike by the side of the highway. Taking off across a fallow field, I pelted the rain with my body.

Soon I emerged from the cloudburst into an oasis between the walls of water. The eye of my storm. The lightning touched the ground there, in the center of this clearing, surrounded by the forest of rain.

As I approached it, I could feel the electricity, prickly heat on my skin, occasional small shocks nipping at me like biting flies. Right up next to it, the air grew dense and I pushed through it, starting to sweat. The lightning hung before me, within my grasp, like a rope thrown down by the higher power to pull me out of this world. It was too bright to look directly at this stalactite, dangling down from a cloud far above, a mass of tendrils and filaments intertwined and shining with the force of a thousand suns.

Just reach out and take hold of this third rail, this downed power line, the voice whispered inside my head. Let it consume you and then disappear.

I had heard that voice before. At the intersection of Jenifer and Wisconsin at 1:17 p.m. on a beautiful Thursday. Michael Stipe had not been the only voice inside my head when I left my dead mother in my house and started walking.

It was not distraction that placed me in front of that Mercedes. If I had been run over, if I had been killed, it would not have been an accident. I saw the car running the light. I stepped off the curb in front of it. It wasn't planned. It wasn't even something I would have admitted to myself at the time. But it is the truth.

That afternoon at that intersection my action would have had no consequences. Or so I believed. My mother was dead. My father was gone. Mackenzie wanted to be free of me. Grace and Carlos seemed to be moving forward nicely into competent adult lives. No one would notice my absence. My death would affect nothing.

I stretched my hand out before me, tantalizingly close to the lightning. In it, I held Grace's note. Two parts of my brain had disconnected from each other: one coveted the lightning while the other had removed the letter from my pocket. I stared at the envelope and knew that I would continue on. Grace did need me. Someday we would compare stories about what we were both doing at that moment when the world stopped, how close we had each come to tumbling forward into the abyss.

I wondered at that moment if I loved Grace. Maybe she loved me. Possibly this moment that I was having with her but without her would be the one that sealed our happy future fate. That conversation about the day we both almost killed ourselves might happen on a couch on a lazy Sunday in a nice house in a suburb while a couple of kids roamed around looking for mischief and we didn't care because everything was right with the world.

I stepped back from the lightning, my decision made. There was an exit. The person we were waiting for would show up. The nausea was mild and controllable.

Despite the fact that my thighs ached and my calves burned and each muscle in my back felt like it was being ripped apart, I returned to my bike and continued on the road to West Virginia.

The Cabin

THE CHANGS' CABIN IS not really a cabin, despite what they call it. It is a house on a lake. A really nice house. Nicer than my house in D.C. But rustic looking, I guess, on the outside. The inside is pretty tricked out. It's not like you're pissing in an outhouse.

Getting there required some relatively complicated directions on back roads after leaving the highway. Luckily, I not only had the Google directions, but Grace had annotated in the margins. Like at the place where Google said turn left and Grace wrote "It's really just the same road so you'll feel like you're going straight." Or where Google said to get on Hemlock Lane, and Grace wrote, "Yes, the dirt road that you don't think is a road." Eventually, I got there.

I was so exhausted when I arrived that I climbed into a hammock that I was pretty sure no one in Grace's family had ever used and fell asleep for what seemed like a really long time. It was strange, I guess, looking back, to think that I had made the journey only to take a nap. But at that moment it felt like arriving there was the culmination of my goal. Really, though, I was scared of what I might find in the house and sleep seemed like the only way to postpone the discovery. I suppose I could have taken a kayak out on the lake, but that would have been really weird.

When I woke up, I ate a couple of granola bars, took a deep breath, and went inside.

The door was unlocked. Someone was here. I almost shouted out Grace's name, but stopped myself. It would have been wishful thinking that could have brought on another bout of temporary insanity. Didn't want to risk it.

I started to search room by room. There were two bedrooms in the lower level that opened out onto the back of the house where a path led to the lake. The rooms were empty. Everything smelled a bit musty and there was a fly frozen in mid-air in the hallway, as if it was hanging from a single strand of spider web. There was also a bathroom down there. I realized that I was most nervous about bathrooms. The ways to kill yourself there would probably involve razor blades and a lot of blood. I stopped and forced all thought from my mind. I would not imagine Grace's death a thousand times in a thousand ways. I couldn't let myself do that.

She wasn't in the bathroom, thankfully. One level down, two to go.

The main level was very open. Standing at the top of the staircase, I could see the living room, the dining area, the kitchen, and out onto the deck. No Grace. Another bathroom. But just a toilet, no bathtub. How bad could that be? I threw the door open. Empty.

Needed to go upstairs. Had to do it. It was time. Grace had to be there.

There was no one in the first two bedrooms. Not surprising. One was the room her parents stayed in on the rare occasions they came to the cabin, and the other was used by guests. I knew she wouldn't be in there. I lingered. I checked the closets, under the beds. I stalled.

There was an office with an uncluttered desk and empty

bookshelves. A couch that folded out into a bed. No Grace.

The bedroom at the end of the cabin, the one that pointed toward the woods, not the lake, that was where Grace and her sister slept. I decided to check the bathroom first. No one in the main part, but the shower curtain was closed. It felt hot in there, a bit steamy, like someone had taken a shower not long before. I couldn't see through the curtain. I put my hand on the edge of it. Then, I yanked it back.

The shower was empty. That was anticlimactic.

Just her bedroom was left. The door was closed. I paused outside in the hall. This felt like the end.

No one was inside.

I was more deliberate in this room. There weren't that many places a person could tuck themselves away, but I checked them all. As if Grace and I were playing a game of hide and seek. I looked in the closet behind a laundry hamper. Under the bed, of course. I moved a table, checking to see if she was squeezed into an impossibly small space back in the corner. I even lifted up a painting on the wall, given the remote possibility that there could be a secret passageway behind it or maybe an open safe (because if there was a locked safe that would be really frustrating).

Nothing. No one. Nada.

I sat back down on the bed. All this time, I was carrying around Grace's note and the thick envelope for Carlos. There was a rope on the bed. Actually more like a thick cord. Someone had been using it for knot-tying practice and managed to create a loop on the end about the size for two fingers. I tossed it out of the way.

I opened the envelope addressed to Carlos and emptied the contents on the bed. Letters. Lots of letters. Each one from Carlos addressed to Grace.

Jealousy flooded over me. In waves, actually. First that he was writing to Grace and making me feel something I didn't know I felt. Second, a brief foray into wondering if he had actually slept with Mackenzie, even though he said he hadn't. That subsided quickly under the third wave, in which I realized I didn't really care what he did with Mackenzie, but that I was pretty damn angry about whatever was going on with Grace even though I had no idea what that was, and until this road trip began I wouldn't even have been able to tell you that I was into Grace and maybe would have said that it was awesome that my two best friends were getting together if that was in fact what was happening.

I attribute the progression of feelings to a growing maturity on my part. Or spending way too much time alone.

Either way, I was pretty sure that Carlos and I were going to have an interesting conversation when he returned from whatever South American country he was in. (I'm now thinking Suriname?) And if I did find Grace, I might kiss her for real this time.

I picked up the top letter on the pile and started to read. I knew that this broke every single unwritten LSGC(AWGWU) code, but I was pretty sure that Grace would forgive me and equally sure Carlos wouldn't.

Carlos' Last Letter to Grace (with Notes in brackets by the Guide's Author)

Darling Grace,
[Really? Darling? That's laying it on a bit thick. But the author can see that coming from Carlos.]

This is the hardest letter I've ever had to write. You are awesome and mean so much to me. No matter what else you feel at the end of this, I need you to know that. [Why is it that everyone realizes how much someone means to them at the moment that that person doesn't mean enough to stick with them? The author has had this experience with Mackenzie; it always seemed that she loved him most at precisely the times she was explaining why she didn't really love him enough.] But I don't think that this is going to work. [At least he didn't drag it out too much. Points for cutting to the chase.]

The last few months [months?!] have been amazing. But with the end of the school year, we are going to spend the summer apart. You have this amazing internship at the Smithsonian—I can't wait to hear about the mollusks! [In a forensic analysis, this letter has been confirmed to be written by Carlos Delgado, who is known to repeat words, particularly "amazing."] You're going to have an awesome time. [Awesome is another often repeated word. Pointing this out may make it sound like Carlos is inarticulate. Of course, this is not true.] Then you'll go to Yale in the fall, where I'm sure you're going to do great things. It is just going to be a long time before we are in the same place again, starting this summer when I'm in Paraguay. [Paraguay! The author knew it was South America.] Long distance relationships are never fair to anyone.

I do love you and always will. This started under such extreme circumstances with graduation and Duck going AWOL on us and all our parents getting a little bit crazy at the same time. Who knew their mid-life crises would synchronize? [The author is feeling bad again about not knowing what was going on with his friends. Of course, he also suspects that none of their parents went as crazy as his dad.]

So it is best that we end this. I don't even have to say let's be friends because I know we always will be. I can't wait to get back to the States and hear about your summer. Maybe this will finally be the time when Duck gets his head out of his feathered ass and realizes that you two were meant to be together (but I'll stop because I know you've heard enough about that from me already). [Whoa.]

Write me if you feel like it, but I'll understand if you don't.

Love,
Carlos

Jump

READING CARLOS' LETTERS TO Grace might lead you to think that whatever action she has taken, whatever urges she has to commit suicide, were due to being hurt by a boy. If you think that, it's because you don't know Grace. That would never be enough to push her over the edge. There are so many things going on in her head. She's complicated. (but then again isn't anyone worth knowing?)

I sat there with the last letter in my hand. I read it again. I kept stopping on Carlos' comment about me getting my head out of my ass. How much had I missed over the years? There was no doubt my feelings for Grace ran deep. But at that moment, I just wanted to find her.

It is so easy to miss important details in the frozen world. Key stimuli are missing. Like a breeze through an open window. When the air doesn't move, the window might as well be closed for all you'll notice. It might also take you longer than it should to realize that the rope you tossed aside when you sat on the bed was someone's failed attempt to make a noose.

The window was the one that faced the side of the house, not the lake. It was wide open, pushed up as far as it would go. Through it, I saw mainly the woods along the side of the house. But when I looked closer, scanning the view like a Find-the-Hidden-Objects puzzle, I found something incongruous. A foot.

Grace's foot. Bare. Toes pointing back toward the room. Her sole facing upward toward the sun.

My first instinct was to grab her ankle and pull her back inside. Thankfully, I usually ignore my first instinct.

Here's what I saw out the window and what I think happened. Grace jumped. I don't know how in the world she decided that was the way to do it, but she must have crouched on the windowsill, put her hands in front of her like a kid learning to dive off the edge of a pool and let herself fall forward. All this happened a moment before the world froze because there she was, head pointed straight down, arms stretched out in front of her. It was a good looking dive. I guess she figured that she'd have to hit the ground head first to do the job. But even so, the act didn't seem well thought out. She could easily break her neck and not die. But there was no other explanation. No one pushed her. She didn't slip. It wasn't an accident.

Grace jumped.

I picked up the rope and I could feel her frustration coursing through it. Grace did not react well to not being good at something. And maybe it turned out that she was lousy at figuring out how to kill herself. When she couldn't tie the noose with the rope she brought, she probably looked for a belt or something else. But the house has almost nothing in it. The medicine cabinets were empty too. No pills to overdose on. She had driven up here, but there was no garage, so death by car exhaust was not an option. And Grace knew way too much about anatomy to slit her wrists. Too painful, and it took too long to bleed out.

So she jumped.

Like I said before, sometimes really smart people do stupid things.

Which brings us back to my first instinct. If I had grabbed her ankle, there was no way I would have been strong enough to pull her up, but I would have gotten her moving, which would have dropped her straight to the ground.

I had to find another way to get her down without hurting her.

From below, the situation looked even worse. Grace was still pretty high up there. I circled the space under her, trying to get a bead on where she'd hit. Made myself a little dizzy. This was all complicated by the fact that that side of the house is built into a hill. No way for her to hit the ground head on. It would always be an angle. The place she was pointed at had a couple of rocks terraced into the hill. Maybe she was aiming for one of those.

I stopped and just stared up into Grace's face. She looked peaceful. Not the expression of screaming terror I would have expected from someone who just jumped out a window. It was probably a fluke of the moment time stopped. She hadn't been out that long. I suspected she was still getting a euphoric rush from falling. That expression would change in another second when the reality set in. But for now, Grace seemed pleased with her choice.

I reached up for her. Our hands weren't even close to each other, a full floor of the house between them. I jumped. Yeah, that got me three inches, after which I slid halfway down the hill. There was a ladder in the garage, but every time I tried to set it up on the incline, it slipped or skidded. I could barely get one step up before the whole operation became unstable.

There was only one way I was going to get to her. I had to go out the same window she did.

I was going to need a lot of mattresses.

This was the point in the movie where you would have a slapstick montage of me dragging mattresses around. Falling over when I pulled them off beds. Tumbling down the stairs with the mattress bouncing along after me. Getting trapped against the wall when a king-size mattress slowly shifted its center of gravity the wrong way, crushing me. All of it would have a bouncy song as accompaniment—something old and catchy and lyrically only somewhat appropriate, like "Talking in Your Sleep" by the Romantics. I wish I could have had a montage because the real work was tedious and painful. Mattresses are really heavy and hard to get a grip on. I fell down a lot. It wasn't funny.

Overall, I dragged six mattresses out of the house. I stacked a double layer of them roughly under where I thought Grace would fall, taking care to make sure the gaps didn't line up. It would suck to do all that work and then have her land between the mattresses on the unforgiving ground.

Of course, since we were on a hill, it was a little tricky to figure out exactly where impact would be and to decide how much coverage the mattresses needed to ensure that she didn't just bounce off and then land on the ground. I ended up getting all the pillows from all the couches as well and creating a secondary perimeter around the core.

In order to do this, I spent a great deal of time looking up at Grace. She was wearing a pair of shorts and a top that maybe you'd call a blouse. I don't know. It was kind of loose fitting and buttoned up the middle. A little lacy around the sleeves. It rose up a bit when she jumped, revealing her midriff. It was a little awkward because I'd be standing there calculating angles and trajectories and trying to decide how fast she would be falling and then I'd just be staring at her bare stomach or walking up the hill in an effort to see if I could get a better look up her blouse, maybe even get a glimpse of bra.

I hadn't really thought things like that before. There were so many girls that you couldn't help but stare at cleavage or bare thigh, and suddenly Grace was one of those girls for me, which is messed up because she was currently hanging in mid-air two stories off the ground, one momentarily frozen world away from breaking her neck. I really needed to focus on the task at hand.

I didn't have enough mattresses.

Cue second montage. Maybe set this one to "I'm So Tired" by Björk. Because by the time I hiked over to the closest neighbor, broke into their house and made six more trips back and forth lugging mattresses, I was exhausted.

Now, I had a pretty good cushion for the plunge. Mattresses four deep with enough coverage by random pillows in every direction to break any secondary fall. I got on top of my creation and jumped. I threw myself down in various places, checking to see where I would bounce. I let myself go over the edge, checking for holes in my safety net. I was ready.

Well, the landing pad was ready. I wasn't. So I lay down on my massive new bed and took a nap.

I woke abruptly from a dream where I was falling toward the mattresses but they turned out to be a cloud, and I dropped right through them, headed toward a certain death.

It was time.

Or so I thought. Until I was back upstairs in Grace's room, looking down two stories at my mattresses on a hill. The surface area to land on appeared much smaller from up here. I leaned farther out the window, which was not a great idea unless I was hoping to sap my courage even more. It was a long way down.

Grace's feet were right in my face. My eyes wandered down her smooth legs to the edge of her shorts, which were billowing just enough to let me see the edge of her panties.

That's enough of that. I snapped back to the task at hand. I needed to get Grace down. Without breaking her neck or mine. Here's what was necessary—a push on her ankles hard enough to get her to land on her back when she hit the mattresses. I was quite sure that I couldn't do that from the angle I had unless I went out the window with her. All a shove from inside would do would change the angle, but she'd still land head first.

However, if I jumped while holding her ankles, the weight of my body and my momentum would pull her far enough for her to land on her back. That was the theory anyway. The key was to do it in such a way that I didn't land on her or break my own neck.

I stared out the window for a long time. Looking at Grace. Tracing paths to the soft surface below. Figuring out angles and trajectories. Knowing there was probably some math to be done, but knowing equally well that I wasn't going to do it.

When I understood with absolute certainty that all my planning probably wouldn't match up with reality, I climbed up on the windowsill. The opening was just wide enough that I was able to press my back against the top with my feet on the bottom, wedged in there in an extremely uncomfortable crouch. For a second, I feared I had gotten myself stuck there. That would be a stupid and slow way to die. But I was able to wriggle forward just enough that I knew I could get out.

I reached out my hands to within inches of Grace's ankles. I was exactly where I needed to be. Time for the leap of faith.

I jumped, pushing off with all of my strength from the bottom of the windowsill. I flew. I grabbed Grace's ankles and then we were both falling forward. I started to rotate sideways and I lost my grip on Grace. That was it. My part (except for the falling) was done. I didn't know if it had been enough. And in a fleeting moment, I thought how awesome it was that at least we were both moving.

Then, I was screaming. All the way down. Until I hit the mattresses on my side and it knocked the wind and all sound clear out of me. I bounced and rolled. Sky, house, mattress, trees, mattress edge, falling, pillows, grass. *Ouch.*

Everything hurt. I couldn't breathe. Maybe I'd broken my ribs and punctured a lung. Then I started to breathe again. Without pain. I was hyperventilating a bit, but I was okay.

Grace. She wasn't on the ground with me. I reached up and

grabbed the top of the wall of mattresses. My shoulder ached, but I pulled myself up anyway.

There she was. On her back looking up at the sky. I scrambled onto the mattresses and over to her. Checked her arms and legs—nothing was at odd angles. The expression on her face had not changed at all. No relief at being down. As far as she know, she was still locked in that first moment of euphoria as she fell.

I kissed her.

Kind of surprised myself with that one. But once I was in, I let myself linger. I might have copped a feel, but if you tell Grace that I'll deny it.

When I finished, I expected Grace to blink and yawn and stretch like a princess awakening from a hundred-year slumber. But no fairy tale ending here.

Discussion: Endings

THE AUTHOR WOULD LIKE to take this opportunity to remind the reader that this is a guidebook to your frozen world. Guidebooks, in general, do not have fairy-tale endings. They are intended to provide the necessary information for the traveler to create his or her own story. When the guidebook has exhausted its knowledge, it just ends. No swelling music or meaningful close-ups. A guidebook is no more about reality than a movie or a novel. A guidebook is meant to be aspirational and inspirational. You're on your own for the reality part.

Seriously, if a guidebook—at least the travel kind—was about reality then each one would end by telling you that it is now time to go back to the airport or the train station or the bus. There would be tedious descriptions about waiting in line to check in. Details on checking your bags and eating crappy terminal food. How to prepare yourself for the long trip home and the inevitable letdown of having your once-in-a-lifetime experience come to a close. Better guidebooks might encourage you to capture your memories in words or pictures, to organize them sooner rather than later so as not to forget. Because there is no fade out at the moment of greatest emotional impact. There is no *The End* just as the main character has reached an epiphany and become a better person. Life continues.

Which is why you may find that the kiss to restart the world does not succeed. You may discover that what you thought was the end of journey actually was not and now you have to ride someone else's bike back to D.C. from West Virginia, except this time you are going to go much slower since you have awkwardly positioned the girl who you now think you might be in love with in the child carrier that you are towing which was clearly meant for someone less than half her size. Back over familiar terrain, roads you have traveled, repeating tasks that you already completed, seeing again things already seen—which no self-respecting guidebook would recommend. You'll cut a new path through sheets of rain. You'll talk to your companion and maybe with her presence some of these experiences will seem new. But since she is as static as the rest of the world, this is not likely. Mainly, you will pedal and maintain your balance and carry on.

This is the conclusion of your practical guide to surviving in a frozen world. From here on out, you're on your own.

Repair the World

EVERY OTHER YEAR AT LSGC(AWGWU), the entire school takes a week off from classes for Religion Week. Basically, the school invites representatives from every religion that they can think of to come and talk to the students in half-hour blocks of time. The religious leaders are urged to focus on commonalities between faiths, which leads to a lot of banal commentary on love and faith and charity and generally being a good person. It was actually a pretty interesting week as far as school weeks at LSGC(AWGWU) went. Though I'll admit I never saw where, say, the Mormons and the Rastafarians had common ground. But maybe I wasn't trying that hard.

One thing I remember from Religion Week in seventh grade was the rabbi who spent the whole time explaining the concept of Tikkun Olam. It means Repair the World. The theory is that we're all in this together and therefore we each need to do our part, preferably a little bit every day, to fix the problems of the world.

That's what I was thinking about as I coasted to a stop in Grace's driveway. It was time for me to put everything back in its place. Right some wrongs and repair the world.

Of course, I was also a sweaty mess from all the biking from West Virginia. I felt a little bad about that when I had to carry Grace back into her house. I started by trying to give her a bear hug, chest to chest, but that felt sleazy and she kept slipping in my arms. Turns out it is also hard to give someone a piggyback ride when they don't hold on. My next option was to sling her over my shoulder, but I nearly dropped her on her head, which would have been particularly annoying given that I had managed to maneuver her into a flawless two-story fall without dropping her on her head. Finally, I ended up cradling her in my arms like a bride being carried over the threshold. It was a struggle, but I only knocked her head against the wall—gently—twice.

By the time I laid her on her back on her bed, I was out of breath and ready for a nap. Some undetermined amount of time later, I woke up next to Grace. I had wrapped an arm across her stomach and nuzzled my face against her side, somewhere between her armpit and breast. That doesn't sound particularly appealing, I know, but she was warm and I woke up smiling for the first time in a long while. That is, until I remembered that her mother was in the room with us sitting at the computer. That really snapped me to attention (and away from her daughter's breasts). Even still, I was well rested and ready to fix what I had broken.

But first I needed to make sure that when Grace came to she didn't go into shock. I took my mother's necklace and clasped around her neck, carefully placing the interlocking rings on Grace's sternum. I took one of her hands and rested it on the chain so there was no way she could miss it. Grace was the only one of my friends who my mom had told the story of the necklace to. She would understand I had been there. That would help, but it wouldn't be enough to keep her confusion and fear from overwhelming her. So I wrote her a note.

That took a long time. I'm not going to tell you what it said. I think I've been pretty clear that it is LSGC(AWGWU) tradition to keep these things secret between the writer and addressee. I found an envelope in her desk drawer and sealed it up. I put my letter in her other hand, having scrawled her name on the front. She will recognize my handwriting—it is like a third grader's.

Outside her house, standing in the perfect 71 degree day, I realized that I had no idea how to put everything I had changed back in place. There was so much I couldn't fix. I couldn't uneat the food or undrink the hundreds of bottles of water. I couldn't unstab the man I had stabbed. (I probably could have undone the damage I'd done at Mackenzie's house, but decided I didn't want to.) So many little things had been changed by me that would remain altered, the thousands of slight adjustments to the world that would be noticed when everyone else came to.

I figured I should pick a couple of big ticket items and do those. Be done with it. Hope it was enough to earn me some brownie points and make the unfreezing transition a little easier for some.

First, I biked methodically block by block everywhere that I could remember going since the world froze. I was looking for all the victims of my people tipping. Whenever I found someone I'd knocked over, I sat them up against the nearest wall and folded their hands in their lap. It seemed to be the best way to get them out of the way and prevent them from coming to more harm. Of course, none of this fixed the real problem, which is that I had no idea whether I had actually hurt these people when I knocked them over in the first place. But I hoped they would wake up a little less disoriented. By the time I was done, most of downtown D.C. looked like a giant conceptual art installation entitled *Sitting In Place*.

My next project took me back out to the shopping mall in Maryland. I had to do something with all that money in the fountain. Unfortunately, like Mr. Zimmerman, I had no idea how much I'd taken from any of those people. My confusion was compounded by the fact that I had at the time thought that Carlos had collected some of the money but Carlos didn't exist so I must have done it all, which I didn't really want to think about. So I would just have to redistribute it another way. The problem is that if all that money was just sitting in that fountain when the world unfroze, there might be a riot as the folks there went for it. I couldn't have that on my conscience. I considered giving equal amounts to the people in the mall, but that might also lead to a bad scene. Time to go Robin Hood.

Nothing had changed at the mall. No one had moved. The money sat in the fountain, undisturbed. I found some duffel bags and dry food containers from the department store. Ones, fives, tens, twenties, fifties, hundreds. Each denomination needed its own carrying case. There were very few fifties and hundreds, so I got a small wallet for each. But the others required different sized bags. There was a period of trial and error as I fit the amount of currency to the space. If a bag was either too full or too empty, I searched the mall for another more appropriate vessel. Each one had to be just right. And soon, I had four well-stuffed bags of varying sizes.

The dry food containers were for the change. Again, pennies, nickels, dimes and quarters got their own receptacles. For some reason I can't explain, the change needed to be visible, almost as if the heft of each container could only be confirmed by seeing the actual coins. Funny that I didn't feel that way about the paper money. This process also took experimentation, until the perfectly sized jars could be obtained. In an unusual display of flexibility, I allowed myself to combine the few half-dollars, silver dollars, Susan B. Anthonys, Sacagaweas and other random cast-offs into a single small cylinder meant for spices.

I filled up my bags and jars, compacting what I had allowed to expand into the fountain. When I was done, all of the money was loaded into the kid carrier, ready to be redistributed.

Parking meters and homeless people. The beneficiaries of my charity. I wasn't sure that plugging the meters would do any good. Might just be a waste of good change. So, each time I saw a meter, I stopped and carefully balanced a quarter on top of it, satisfied that it would be put to good use by a harried parker. It took some thought to decide how much to give each homeless person I encountered. I finally settled on one hundred dollars doled out in neat little packets. A hundred felt like a perfect round number that might be viewed by some of the recipients as an act of divine intervention. In my mind, I imagined that I was inspiring people to turn their lives around through my small infusion of cash. I tried not to listen to that tiny cynical voice that nattered on about enriching the pockets of local liquor stores and drug dealers.

When I ran out of parking meters and homeless people, I gave all the rest of the money to a food bank that LSGC(AWGWU) had once taken us to for a community service project. I lined up the bags at the front door like babies abandoned at the gates of an orphanage. I wrote a note asking that they use the money wisely and signed it *Anonymous*.

That was all the cash, except for the pennies.

I took my jar of pennies to the Capitol reflecting pool. I took one out and tossed it in a high arc into the water. Ripples fanned out from the point of impact. Everything those waves touched moved. The sunlight on the surface shimmered. The Capitol Building shook. The reflected tourists, taking a break from their long hot day in this cool space, danced. I looked down on myself, distorted. But, soon enough, the water returned to its natural state—calm, glassy, dead.

Another coin, more waves. And again and again and again. Penny by penny by penny. I threw them everywhere in the pool, trying to space the sparkling jewels out evenly. I was working toward something or possibly nothing.

This was all coming to an end, but like the jar of pennies, I wasn't really sure what I would have when it was empty.

With each coin, with each splash, with each new set of expanding concentric circles, I made a wish. All variations on a theme.

Let them move. Let her move. Let her live. Let this come true. Let me be right. Let me understand. Let her understand. Let her believe. Let us go.

I thought about me and my father sitting on the boat-car in the middle of this pool. The last time that time stopped. We lay there on the benches, waiting to be captured or rescued. Or not really waiting for anything. Ignoring the tyranny of time. Not thinking. Not caring. It was a perfect moment. There are so few of those and standing there throwing money into this wishing well, I wanted it back.

Then the jar was empty. The water stopped moving. The pennies papered the fountain floor. I expected them to glitter like gold, but it was just a layer of dull copper brown.

One More Time to St. Es

THE ROOM AND MY father were exactly how I'd left them. Something about these halls—the light in this place—made Saint Elizabeths seem even more abandoned than the world surrounding it.

I noticed the scraggly growth on his face. Not a beard or even a potential one. Someone was shaving him, just not often or particularly well. There was a brownish smudge on his chin. Chocolate or maybe gravy. His eyes were crusty in the corners, filled with unattained sleep.

The words called to me. I focused on the walls, scanning over the sheer volume and scope. So many words. So many possibilities. If only they could be put into order, rearranged, there must be meaning here.

It could be done. Of course it could. My father's message to me could be the answer to everything. The key to unlock the world. I just needed to organize his thoughts. I would finish what he started. And it would all be okay.

But how to do it? Obviously, all the words needed to be torn from the walls. Gathered in one place, a massive pile in the empty corner. Then organized. Scraps that contained a single word would be easy. Greater attention would be paid to words that had been cut out multiple times. But what of phrases? Divide them up by number of words first. One, two, three, four, five, etc. Then alphabetize by first word? Would that be useful? Or was there a way to partition them by meaning or subtext? No, start with the words themselves. Keep it simple. Alphabetize. Once the words covered the floor in accessible patterns, then they would be ready to return to the walls. But in order, a narrative this time. I would tell a story and in turn the story would tell my future. Magical runes that would prophesy my next move, my road out of this world. It would take a long time, but it would tell me what I was supposed to do. My purpose.

This is my purpose.

Isn't it?

"No."

I spun around. The voice had surprised me. For a moment, panic swept through me. I stopped breathing. If I started hallucinating my father moving, I probably wouldn't be able to take it. But my father had not spoken.

I realized that the voice had been my own. Yeah, that's less crazy.

"No," I said again aloud, just to test if it was the same voice I had heard moments earlier. It sounded alien. I had no idea the last time I had spoken.

No, this was not my purpose. Those words on the walls did not belong to me. They were not my answers; they were his. Nothing I did in this room would unfreeze the world.

I finally understood.

Out at the nurse's station, one of the orderlies had a bottle of water. I tipped it over onto a washcloth, soaking it through. I returned to my father's room and washed his face. The dirt and grit transferred easily from his chin, his cheeks, his eyes, to the square of cloth in my hand. I found a towel by his bed and dried him off.

That done, I pulled a chair over from the wall and sat across from him at the table.

He looked at me. I was the person he had been waiting for. Now here I was and I detected the hint of a smile on his face.

My regrets were sharp. I laid them out on the table between us like a deck of cards.

"Mom is dead," I said. "It happened this morning."

When my mother got sick, I wrote my father a letter. It was an epic letter, full of flowery and ornate language, complex sentences with interlocking clauses that tripped over themselves, ambitious leaps of logic and intricate digressions. The style paid homage to my father's own prose, dense and often unmanageable. I needed for him to see who I was, what I had become—an equal, a peer. I longed to create an impression of a formidable mind and a compassionate soul. I wanted to embody his theories about the self, to confirm his views of the universe. Through tragedy, I would bring truth.

The letter should have said, simply, "Your wife has a tumor and is going to die. I thought you should know."

I should have delivered it in person. I suspected that the letter had never been read. Maybe he had gotten it. Maybe he had cut it up like one of his magazines. It could be that my words were scattered among those on the walls, robbed of any sense or impact.

"I'm sorry ...."

I listened to my voice trail off. How to explain what my apology meant? Sitting there, I knew what I should have done. She had not seen him in years, just like me. Sure, she kept tabs on him, mainly to know if he was about to be released or to find out if he had died. But it had been a long time since either of us had made the trip across the river to visit, to remind ourselves of the connection between us. And all that time, now I knew, he sat there and waited. So what should I have done? When she had started to fade away from herself, but before she was completely gone, I should have brought her to him. My father and mother deserved to say goodbye to each other and I had failed them both. That was my apology.

"The funeral is tomorrow," I said.

I had failed. But not completely. There was time to reconcile, time to repent. There was time.

"I'll come get you. We'll go together."

I didn't know how that would happen. I just knew that it would.

Tomorrow.

Tomorrow

I RETURNED THE BIKE and carrier to the boy and his father eating their picnic in the park. From there, I was on foot. I walked back to my mother's house. That was where I needed to start. Steps needed to be retraced.

It took me a while to remember the last place I had put my phone. It had become such a useless object. But I had to have that too. It was on the kitchen table, waiting.

I jammed the earbuds in, shutting out the silence of the world around me, filling my head with a different kind of silence. Standing on my mother's doorstep, I took a deep breath and began to walk.

It was so long ago, but I made sure that I took exactly the same path. If I had sidestepped a piece of gum on the sidewalk, then I did that again. If I had been forced to wait at a corner, I paused in the same place and counted to ten before I let myself continue.

I wanted to run. But instead I passed through these streets at the same pace I had before. A steady determined gait. A last purposeful walk.

Not everything was the same. Though I wore the same

clothes and had my phone, I was not the same person. I tried to think about what my thoughts had been at that time, but that was something I was unable to recreate. Those were lost to me forever. Time had dulled my grief and anger.

I arrived at the intersection of Wisconsin and Jenifer. Nothing had changed. The three bystanders were still there, and we all considered the Mercedes about to run the red light.

Taking a deep breath, I stepped back into the intersection. I took my place once more in front of the bumper.

This is how it is supposed to be. This is my intervention.

I closed my eyes. I thought about my mother and my father. I thought about Carlos and Grace, and Grace and me. I thought about the end of high school and the beginning of college. I thought about turning eighteen and dying. I let the darkness surround me and I did not move.

But only for a moment.

Without opening my eyes, I took a step backward. Tentative at first, but the second step was more confident. I knew where my feet had been planted before and I walked in those same footsteps again in reverse. I smiled when my heel hit the curb. I lifted myself back up onto the sidewalk.

I don't know what sound I heard first. Maybe all at once.

The blast of the Mercedes engine. The scream of its brakes. The rush of air as it flew by. The gasp of the tearful woman next to me. The accented voice of the messenger: "Damn, man." The taco truck guy making change. The bus pulling up to the curb across the street. And more distant, stretching out forever, sirens, jackhammers, laughter, everything.

My phone came back to life in my hand. I sang the R.E.M. lyrics and Michael Stipe sang with me.

"Begin the begin."

The song ended.

I stood there on the corner, with my eyes still closed, and I waited for the light to change and another song to begin.

Questions for Book Clubs

1. If you were the only person moving in a world where time stopped, what would you do first?

2. Which of Duck's personality traits would make him more likely to survive than most in this situation? Can you imagine how you yourself might react?

3. Duck enjoys certain aspects of his frozen world. What would you do to amuse yourself?

4. If you were writing the Guide to Your Frozen World for where you live, what would be the top attractions to visit in a world where time stopped and what would you do there that you can't do under normal circumstances?

5. Can you think of any explanation, rational or mystical, for what is happening to Duck? Do you think time froze because of a single moment in Duck's life? Or was it completely random?

6. Duck's father's philosophy includes a statement that actions are only moral in reference to how they are viewed by other people. In other words, if no one is there to judge you, then there is no such thing as right and wrong. Do you agree? Can there be immorality without feedback from other people?

7. Duck has opportunities to be a vigilante. But he isn't quite sure that his reads of the situations are correct. If you were in his shoes, would you act if you thought a crime was being committed? How sure would you have to be?

8. Is Duck's predicament a blessing or a curse?

9. Does this story remind you of other books or movies you have enjoyed? Why?

MICHAEL LANDWEBER IS the author of the novel, *We* (Coffeetown Press, 2013). His stories have appeared in *American Literary Review, Gargoyle, 14 Hills, Fugue, The MacGuffin* and other places. He is an associate editor at *Potomac Review* and a contributor to *Pop Matters* and *Washington Independent Review of Books*. Mike lives in Washington D.C. with his wife and two children.

Find out more at www.mikelandweber.com.

Also by Michael Landweber from Coffeetown Press:

If you could talk to your childhood self, would that child listen?

we

A NOVEL

THE ERIC HOFFER AWARD
FINALIST

MICHAEL LANDWEBER

After an accident, 40-year-old Ben regains consciousness in the house he grew up in. Ben has become a psychic hitchhiker in the brain of his younger self, 7-year-old Binky, who is not happy to have him there. It is 3 days before a vicious attack on his sister that will scar Ben's family forever. Even if Ben can get Binky to say the right words, who will believe a boy can foretell the future?